THEIR CRAMPED DARK WORLD AND OTHER TALES

by
David A. Riley

Parallel Universe Publications

First Published in 2015 by Hazardous Press
This edition Parallel Universe Publications
Copyright © 2015 David A. Riley

Hoody was first published in *When Graveyards Yawn*, Crowswing Books, 2006

A Bottle of Spirits was first published in *New Writings in Horror 2*, Sphere Books, 1972

No Sense in Being Hungry, She Thought was first published in *Peeping Tom* #20, 1996

Now and Forever More was first published in *The Second Black Book of Horror*, Mortbury Press, 2008

Romero's Children was first published in *The Seventh Black Book of Horror*, Mortbury Press, 2012

Swan Song was first published in *The Ninth Black Book of Horror*, Mortbury Press, 2012

The Farmhouse was first published in *New Writings in Horror*, Sphere Books, 1971

The Last Coach Trip was first published in *The Eighth Black Book of Horror*, Mortbury Press, 2011

The Satyr's Head was first published in *The Satyr's Head and Other Tales of Terror*, Corgi Books, 1975

Their Cramped Dark World was first published in *The Sixth Black Book of Horror*, Mortbury Press, 2010

ISBN: 978-0-9574535-9-3
Parallel Universe Publications, 130 Union Road,
Oswaldtwistle, Lancashire, BB5 3DR, UK

For Linden

CONTENTS

Hoody   7

A Bottle of Spirits   25

No Sense in Being Hungry, She Thought   35

Now and Forever More   43

Romero's Children   71

Swan Song   85

The Farmhouse   109

The Last Coach Trip   119

The Satyr's Head   133

Their Cramped Dark World   171

HOODY

Laurence Huxtable left the tube station with his usual feeling of relief at having got away from the claustrophobic depths of its cramped tunnels, teeming crowds and endless flights of stairs and escalators. He hated the tube, but from where he lived in London it would take too long to travel to work by bus, and he could not afford to run a car, even without the crippling congestion charges in the centre.

His canvas shoulder bag securely tucked beneath one arm, Laurence marched up the slope at Highgate Station to the main road above with a spring in his heels, almost welcoming the sights and sounds: the ceaseless streams of traffic along Archway and the lights of the shops and offices that rose around him. Anything was better than the neon-lit tunnels he had left behind for the weekend. During the next two days the only travelling he would be do would be by foot to his local pub or the convenience store.

It was already dark and the slope to the main road was littered with dried leaves from the small parkland to the left. They crunched beneath his feet with a satisfying crispness.

There was nothing quite like the weekend, especially when he was up to date with his work at the design office and he had none to take home with him. There was a nearly full bottle of Bushmills in the cupboard and a six-pack of Fosters in the fridge, while tucked in his bag were a couple of DVDs he bought in HMV during his lunch break. Which meant, he thought with a feeling of satisfaction, that tonight was sorted. While tomorrow night there would be a session at the Winchester with Alec and Daz and his girlfriend Liz after a day washing and ironing and all the other chores that built up during the week.

It was with these thoughts running through his mind that Laurence approached the main road, passing the last of the parked cars. A bus rumbled past along the road, its motion drawing his attention, when he glimpsed a hooded figure stood on the other side of the narrow car park. Laurence was not normally nervous or paranoid about other people, even on the tube, despite the suicide bombings in July, but for a moment he felt a tremor of what felt like fear as he glimpsed the tall, dimly-seen man. It was not that there was anything peculiar or even distinctive in what the man wore: dark grey tracksuit bottoms and a zipped-up top, with a hood that covered most of his face. Laurence didn't care for hoodies. It was a fashion style too medieval and drab for his tastes. Not that his own fashion sense was particularly flamboyant. But there was something just a tad too plain and utilitarian about hoodies. Not to mention the sometimes-worrying anonymity their headgear gave them. Especially attractive to shoplifters, he'd heard. And muggers.

Laurence squared his shoulders and straightened his back, conscious that he had been the only passenger to alight from his train and there was no one else behind him, though there were only a couple of yards to go before he reached ground level.

But the hoody did not move. Perhaps there was nothing sinister about him, just a young lad waiting till his girlfriend arrived. Laurence smiled to himself as he left the car park and headed down Archway, weaving his way through the pedestrians packed along the pavement, amused at himself at his senseless alarm, even though more than one of his friends had been too complacent on occasion and ended up being mugged. The streets of London were not as safe as all that. And a degree of caution sometimes had to be exercised if you wanted to avoid that kind of trouble.

The rest of the journey home was uneventful, and he was soon in his first floor flat above Le Bistro Bleu, the smell from its kitchen whetting his appetite as he raced upstairs and fished for his keys. Tonight, would be pizza from Ali's takeaway down the street, while he settled down to a couple of movies.

By half eleven he had watched both DVDs and was bleary-eyed and ready for bed. The living room windows looked out over the blue awning of the bistro below. As he gazed down, prior to closing the curtains, he saw that the street was busy as usual for a Friday night with crowds outside the Red Dragon Pub. Alcohol-heightened laughter echoed between the terraced buildings. Though most people were gathered in groups of varying sizes, from a raucous hen party of a dozen very drunken girls to threes and fours, there was a figure conspicuously by himself, stood on the unlit doorstep of a computer shop, its windows sealed behind alloy blinds. Laurence felt a twinge of apprehension when he recognised the hoody he saw outside the tube station. Or, he corrected himself, since he had been able to see no more of the man's face then than now, someone in the same kind of grey tracksuit bottoms and zipped up top, with the hood pulled down over his face. Of course, it could have been someone else altogether. The clothes were hardly distinctive. They were about as anonymous as you could get these days. But there was something about the man, perhaps the extreme stillness with which he stood on the shop's doorstep, the posture of his body, the slight inclination of his head, which left barely any of his face visible beneath the hood, which reminded Laurence of the man he saw earlier. He wondered how much time the poor sod spent hanging around like this, waiting for someone to turn up. *If* he was waiting for someone, of course. Perhaps he had nothing better to do. Or nowhere to go. Perhaps he was homeless. Though that wasn't the impression Laurence had. He'd seen plenty of homeless people in London and could recognise them straight away. This guy didn't look like any of them. It was hard to explain but there was something about the figure that Laurence found disturbing, as if the man was only there on account of him. Was he watching the flat? The doorstep he was on was a only short distance down the street, but he didn't appear to be looking this way. If anything, he was angled too far away to have a clear view of the bistro either, especially with the hood blocking most of his field of vision.

Laurence decided he was being paranoid. It was hardly coincidental that someone he saw only a mile away at the tube station should be stood on this particular street, with all its pubs, cafes, takeaways and shops. Even if, he reminded himself with an attempt at realism, it was the same person.

Laurence shut the curtains and turned off the lights. By the time he was in his bedroom the figure was all but forgotten as he tumbled, tiredly, into bed.

*

The next morning Laurence was out by nine on his way to the mini market at the end of the block for a carton of milk for his breakfast and a morning paper. It was a sunny day, with just a hint of autumn in the air, the sky as clear as it ever got in London.

He was surprised to see a police incident van parked down the street. Several policemen stood outside Computer Express, the pavement taped off for several yards on either side. As he passed by on the opposite pavement he glanced across and saw a large pool of what looked like dried blood on the paving stones outside the shop. A very large pool.

Wishing that he hadn't looked, Laurence hurried on.

*

"Why didn't you say anything?" Liz said, her voice raised against the deafening clamour of a Heavy Metal record someone had put on the juke box. Her bleached blond hair had been cut short in the last week and she looked uncannily like a judge as she stared over their drinks at him, her thin face set in a scowl. "It's disgusting. Too many people ignore what's going on these days. No wonder the country's in the state it is. When was the last time you stopped to put money in a charity box or bothered to buy a copy of *The Big Issue*?"

"Hey, I do my bit," Laurence said in protest.

A social worker and a part-time volunteer at Shelter, Liz was so uptight about things like this, that he knew he should have had more sense than mention it to her. "Anyway, I didn't see anything that could help the police."

"You don't know that," Liz said. "Anything might help them find who knifed the man."

"If it was him."

"And how many guys did you see last night with a hood pulled over their heads, standing only a few yards from your flat on their own?"

Laurence shrugged, took a gulp of his lager and wished either Alec or Daz or their two girlfriends would say something, but they knew Liz too well to get involved. Lights from the bandit next to them reflected off the stainless-steel pins threaded through her left eyebrow as she continued to stare at him, making her look for a moment like a terminator with part of its endoskeleton showing through. Laurence took a second gulp of his lager. That was no way to look at your girlfriend, he thought. She'd crucify him if he mentioned that to her!

"I'll probably have a word on the phone to someone tomorrow," he said.

"Any chance of upgrading *probably* to *will*?" Liz asked.

"I'll *will* have a word on the phone to someone tomorrow?" Alec mimicked with a grin almost as broad as his stomach. A northerner, he had a high-pitched Liverpool accent which somehow let him get away with statements for which any of the others would have been well and truly roasted.

"And when did being a grammar Nazi become a scouse type of thing?" Liz asked.

"I thought us scousers were renowned for it."

The mood lightened, for which Laurence was relieved. Admittedly, the report in *The Evening Standard* about the man who'd been stabbed to death, had been a shock. About which Liz had done little to make him feel any better.

From the brief report in the newspaper the attack must have happened only minutes after he looked onto the street last night. No one saw the attack. The first anyone seemed to know anything about it was when the man collapsed, bleeding. By the time an ambulance arrived he was already dead.

Liz stayed over at Laurence's flat that night. Since they started going out two years ago, she had been adamant she would only stay at his place one night a week. She valued her independence too much to consider living together. In turn he could stay at her place too. One night a week.

It was a case of like it or lump it.

In a way it had worked out fine for both of them. Liz could be irritatingly abrasive and, though he suspected that he loved her and that she loved him, they were both too idiosyncratic to give much in the way of compromise, Liz much less than him.

Having Liz with him Saturday night helped take Laurence's mind off the murder, though he knew that Liz would make sure he fulfilled his agreement to have a word with someone on Sunday about it. And perhaps he should, he thought. It might help take away some of the guilt he felt at what had happened.

In the event his phone call to the police was anti-climactic. He was passed on to a DC Trubshaw who thanked him for what little he could tell them about the incident and said that they would appreciate him calling into the station to make a formal statement sometime, but Laurence could tell that his information was far from important. He almost felt like telling Liz "I told you so", but he knew better than to say something like that.

Sunday continued to worsen. Around midday Liz had a call on her mobile from her sister in Brighton to say that their father had been taken ill and been rushed to hospital. This resulted in a series of phone calls to check on the trains from London to Brighton, and with Liz making off to her flat in Muswell Hill for some clothes to take with her.

"I'll get in touch later," she promised as she hurried to her taxi.

Laurence's flat felt barren after Liz had gone. By two o'clock he decided he was too bored to stay in, so he grabbed a coat and rang Alec, who said he was at a loose end too. They arranged to meet at the Winchester for a few pints. The few pints evolved into five, with burgers and chips to help sober them up at tea time, then more pints till, by nine in the evening, they both felt they had had more than enough and strolled to Laurence's flat, with a detour for kebabs on the way. They watched a film on television, then Alec ordered a taxi home.

By half eleven, a couple of coffees after Alec had finally gone, Laurence decided he would go to bed. The after affects of the beers and a phone call from Liz at the hospital in Brighton to tell him things were looking bad and that her father had suffered a major stroke and might not last the night, left Laurence feeling physically drained, and it was with an effort that he took himself to the window to close the curtains.

A figure stood further down the street by the recently scrubbed pavement outside Computer Express made him start. Sober again and very much awake, Laurence stared at the hoody. It was him, he was sure, just as sure as he could feel the cold panes of glass beneath his hands as he craned forward and stared at the motionless figure. His breath misted on the window pane as he tried to remember what the man he saw last night had looked like. Was it the same person? There was the same lack of movement, the same peculiar stillness of the figure, like the one he saw earlier at the tube station. There were even the same slightly darker tracksuit bottoms. The same inclination of the head. The same height, too, perhaps five foot ten or eleven. The same nondescript, dark grey footwear.

Laurence pushed himself back from the window.

It was ridiculous, he thought. He was becoming obsessed. And he couldn't understand why.

Laurence sat down for a moment to compose his thoughts and think things through. Was this how becoming obsessed began? Or worse, was this how becoming paranoid began, twitching at imagined coincidences?

Laurence returned to the window. Disturbingly, the hooded figure was still outside the shop, so motionless he seemed hardly real. A prickle of fear ran down Laurence's spine. This was the start of paranoia, wasn't it? Could he even be sure it wasn't an illusion, that he wasn't making shapes out of shadows, that there was nothing there except a patchwork of light and dark that his imagination had reconfigured into something sinister?

Of course, there was a solution. He could go downstairs and confront whoever was stood outside the shop. But what would he say if there was someone there? And wouldn't it be stupid, perhaps even dangerous? The man might be on drugs. Or a thief just waiting for the street to become quiet before breaking into one of the shops. Or a waiting mugger. Now that would be brilliant, to go up to someone who was hanging around for an opportunity to mug some helpless passer by!

Laurence sighed. Liz would be ashamed of him. There was no way she would get herself wound up over something as senseless as this.

On an impulse Laurence slung on a jacket. Moments later he unlocked the ground floor door next to the bistro and was out on the street. A wind cut through the light jacket he'd put on as he looked towards the computer shop; its neon logo flickered in the dull glow of the lamp posts.

The hoody was still there, as motionless as before. There were perhaps half a dozen people along the street, most of them hurrying, probably home. For a moment Laurence hesitated, his resolve weakening. Then the hoody turned his head towards him, most of his face still hidden apart from the lower part of his jaw.

"Excuse me!" Laurence called, ragging himself even as he said it. What a weak, ineffectual, *la-di-da* kind of thing to come out with, he thought.

Abruptly, the hoody stepped onto the pavement and started striding away from him, hands in the pockets of his top.

Laurence launched himself after him, walking briskly.

"Excuse me!" he said, more loudly this time.

Even at the pace he'd set, the hoody was moving faster, leaving him behind. Weirdly, he didn't even seem to be striding all that quickly either. Laurence increased his speed, almost breaking into a trot, but he could barely keep pace even then.

"Excuse me!"

Whether he heard Laurence or not, the hoody took no notice

of him. Head down, he strode purposefully towards the end of the block, then disappeared around the corner.

"Buggerin' hell," Laurence muttered. He had not meant to turn this into a chase. Now that it had started, though, it did not take that much of an effort to keep going. A few seconds later he rounded the corner as well, surprised to see how far the hoody had managed to walk in the meantime. A tree-filled public garden stood on the far side of the street behind ornamental railings that probably dated back to Edwardian days. Even the lamp posts had the same period look. The hoody had almost reached the end of the garden now. Laurence ran a few strides in an effort to catch up as the man disappeared around another corner, hidden by the trees that were crowded against the railings.

This was a quieter area and for the first time Laurence began to have misgivings. Despite the lamp posts there were too many patches of darkness here. And too many of the buildings were offices, closed for the night. A mugger's paradise. Slowing his pace, Laurence approached the end of the garden more cautiously, edging away from the railings towards the kerb so that he would have a clearer view around the corner. Again, though, the hoody had kept going, and by now had reached an alley that ran along the back of a block of shops.

Laurence slowed to a stop as he watched the hoody stride out of sight down the alley. This was too bloody dangerous, he thought. He was being led like a lamb to the slaughter and he'd be stupid if he fell for it. The alley, with its wheelie bins and piles of empty cardboard boxes, deep doorways and parked vans, was just too dark for him to risk going down in pursuit. If the guy had a knife – or any kind of weapon at all – he'd be in deep trouble.

Deciding that he had taken this as far as was safe, Laurence returned to his flat, a deep feeling of dissatisfaction and an even deeper feeling of disquiet unsettling him.

*

"They said father'll probably be sent home later this week," Liz said on his mobile the following morning. "I've told Karen I'll stay on. He's not out of danger yet and there could be a relapse. I'd never forgive myself if I wasn't here."

"At least there's a chance he could be on the mend." Laurence said in an effort to sound encouraging.

"As far as he'll ever be. He isn't a well man and he'll never be quite the same again, whatever happens."

Laurence had decided not to mention anything about what happened last night. Compared to her grief over her father's illness it would sound petty. And, despite some disjointed nightmares about it when he went to bed, he couldn't help but feel that it probably was.

"Please keep me up to date," he said to her. "If anything happens I can always take some time off work and join you."

"Thanks," Liz said, sounding uncharacteristically touched by his offer. "I appreciate that, Laurie. I really do."

For lunch he called into Starbucks for cappuccino and a Danish pastry, while mulling over a couple of design concepts he'd been working on. The only spare seat was inside the front window. He was sat there gazing at the traffic outside while he drank his coffee when someone stopped on the pavement and stared at him. The shock almost made him choke, and he spluttered coffee into his hand as he stared back at the shadowy face of the hoody, only the narrow, slightly pointed tip of the man's chin and an impression of his eyes visible beneath the hood. The incident lasted barely more than a couple of seconds before the man stepped back. By the time Laurence had recovered enough to put down his coffee and stand up the man had merged into the crowds and gone. The after effect of it didn't die down quite so quickly, though, and Laurence felt jangled all afternoon when he got back to work, where he found it all but impossible to concentrate on what he was doing. What had so far been a vague uneasiness about the hoody had suddenly become frighteningly personal. He told himself that he shouldn't have gone out last night to confront the man, that this might somehow have led to what happened today. Though he could not ignore the suspicion that the fact he had seen the man again and again over the past few days might have been leading up to what happened at Starbucks whatever he did.

On the way home that night he felt nervous, watching the rest of his fellow passengers on the tube for sight of the man. By the time he reached Highgate Station Laurence was so wired up that he almost deliberately stayed on the train till it reached the next stop to avoid the slope that would take him up to the main road. Only the sight of other passengers disembarking at the same time gave him the confidence to get off too, though he stuck as close as he could to them all the way to street level, studiously avoiding looking towards the other side of the car park where the hoody stood on Friday night. Only when he reached Archway did he feel safe, though he walked home quicker than he had ever done before, not satisfied till the ground floor door had been locked behind him. He stood there for several seconds, breathing heavily, his pulse throbbing in his ears. Feeling ashamed of himself at his reaction to the incident and his sudden fear of the hoody, Laurence climbed the stairs to his flat.

Liz rang a short while later. Her father had made a brief recovery during the afternoon, becoming quite chatty. She mentioned telling him about Laurence's offer to take some time off himself to help. Laurence had always got on well with her father, a retired sub-editor on a national newspaper, who had an abiding interest in computers and found Laurence's work on using them for designing artwork fascinating – more so than he did most of the time.

"I'm worried about him," Liz added. "Karen says she's heard that people in his condition sometimes make recoveries like this, then worsen afterwards."

"Your sister's a glass half empty type of person," Laurence told her.

Liz agreed. "But she might be right this time. Anyway, Dad told me to send you his love. He hopes you're well." Liz laughed cheerlessly. "He's desperately ill and he's hoping you're well. Ironic, isn't it?"

That was typical of her father, though, Laurence thought, sharing her sadness at what might well be the man's last illness. After she had rung off, Laurence did not feel like watching TV, preparing himself something simple to eat, then slumped on his sofa, too tired to bother about anything except stare at the wall opposite.

Some time later his phone rang again. This time it was Alec.

"Have you heard the news about that hoody who was murdered on your street? Paul Gilligan, the police called him."

Laurence said that he hadn't. "Liz rang about her dad and I haven't felt like watching the news. Too depressing," he said.

"Depressing or not, you'll find this interesting. When the guy's relatives entered his flat in Wood Green to sort through his stuff they found he'd been storing body parts inside his freezer. Word is that Gilligan had started on a murder spree. It's suspected he was responsible for several murders in different parts of London. Knifings, ironically, considering how the bastard died. The police have been hunting him for months. The main clue, which they'd been keeping to themselves, they say to stop copy cat killings, was that he cut off his victims' thumbs. It was these he'd been storing in his freezer."

"And his killer? Have they said anything about him?"

"It was a gang. Queer bashing. The police think they took him for a gay. Things got out of hand when he pulled a knife on them. A couple of them had knives as well." Alec chuckled. "Anyway, looks like they saved some other poor sod he was eying up for his next victim, eh? Who knows, that might've been you." Which seemed to tickle Alec's sense of humour somehow.

Later that night Laurence turned on the local news on TV. The picture that was flashed up of Paul Gilligan, taken months ago, showed a thin faced man in his mid-twenties with deep, sad-looking eyes and a distinctive pointed chin. A chin which Laurence knew he had seen only hours ago outside Starbucks.

Laurence felt a stab of tension in the back of his head as he

18

stared at the photo. It couldn't be the same man he saw at lunchtime, he knew. It had to have been a coincidence, bizarre though it seemed. No other explanation fitted.

*

The following day Laurence went to work as usual. He had decided to try and put the hoody out of his mind. His growing obsession was probably making him see everyone who wore clothes even remotely similar to the ones he saw last week as a replica of him, even if they weren't. What was happening over Liz's father was far more important, and he knew that he should be thinking about that, as well as finishing his project at work.

He had only been at the office a few minutes, though, when he received a phone call from DC Trubshaw.

"I'm sorry I haven't had time to call in and give a statement yet," Laurence said when the policeman spoke to him.

"I'd be glad if you could get that done sometime soon," Trubshaw told him. "Though that's not why I'm phoning you. It's to see if there's a chance you might remember some of the faces of the other people in the area when you saw Gilligan. We have a number of suspects for the group that attacked him. Even though we've nailed him as a serial killer, Gilligan's death's still murder, and we intend to get whoever was responsible for it."

"I understand," Laurence said, though he wished he could be allowed to forget all about it. "When would you like to see me?"

"If you're free around lunchtime, perhaps you could nip into the station then."

It was drizzling by the time Laurence arrived at the police station. The fine weather had ended, and the sky was a continuous bank of dark, miserable-looking clouds. Depressed already, the drab surroundings of the police station made Laurence feel even gloomier as he waited for the desk sergeant to contact DC Trubshaw.

A plump, round faced man with a heavy moustache and a balding head, Trubshaw had the florid complexion of a heavy drinker, though his dark brown eyes held a disconcerting intensity which told Laurence that, appearances to one side, this was not someone to mess about with.

Trubshaw shook Laurence's hand with a tight grip, then led him to an interview room, its off-white walls and flaking paintwork doing nothing to lift his depression.

"These are a few pictures of some of our suspects," Trubshaw said as a placed a lever-arch book in front of him. Laurence scanned the photographs inside, though none were familiar to him. After twenty minutes he shook his head. "The more I look at them the less I feel sure I'd be able to remember anyone at all," he said.

Trubshaw nodded. "Just keep looking. It's surprising what sometimes rings a bell."

There was a knock at the door. Trubshaw heaved himself up and answered it. Laurence heard him exchange a few comments with someone outside, then a muttered curse. Intrigued, Laurence tried to make out what was being said, when Trubshaw returned. "Bear with me a moment." He took the book from Laurence's hands and flicked through it, then laid it open in front of him again. "This one doesn't ring a bell, does he?"

A blond, stubbly face with staring eyes and a twisted nose, the youth on the photo looked tough and belligerent, with tightly-drawn lips and a hint of a supercilious sneer.

Laurence studied the face intently, unsure. It was memorable enough. "He might have been there. Outside the Red Dragon. I think he was laughing," he went on, surprised how the image flashed back to him. "He was wearing a black leather jacket. There were four, perhaps five others."

Trubshaw nodded. "You're sure?" he asked.

"As sure as I can be," Laurence said. "Why?"

The policeman sighed. "The more that happens the odder the all thing becomes. We suspected this guy." He tapped the youth's photo with a thick, nicotine-stained finger. "One of our patrols went to pick him up from the estate he lives on to be brought in for questioning. It took longer than expected as he wouldn't answer his door. Finally, someone noticed a foot sticking out from behind a chair in the front room of his flat. It could only just be seen through the window. Which gave our men enough grounds to break open the door and go in." Trubshaw shook his head. "Which is when they found him, knifed to death."

Laurence felt the blood drain from his face. "Who did it?" he asked, though the question seemed absurd at this stage.

Trubshaw looked him in the eye. "I shouldn't perhaps be telling you this, but God knows what harm it can do." His brows knitted into a tight frown as he said: "To all intents and purposes Paul Gilligan did it. It bears all the hallmarks of the murders we assumed he committed after finding those thumbs in his freezer. Even the thumb off Slattery's right hand had been removed. Within the last few hours. But Paul Gilligan's been dead for days. So, who did it? And whoever killed Slattery, did he do the other murders too?"

*

Laurence left DC Trubshaw a troubled man with a re-opened case and the question of why Paul Gilligan had five severed dead men's thumbs in his freezer. And who was it who really carried out the murders and cut them off?

Laurence was sick of it all and wished he had never become involved with it. Back at the office he found it impossible to concentrate on his work and when Liz rang to say that her father wasn't expected to last the night he took the opportunity to book the rest of the week off work.

All it needed, as he headed for the tube to go home and pack a bag, was to see the headline on the evening paper: "Black Magic Link To Serial Killer". And, though he knew he should have ignored it, he could not resist buying a copy to read on the tube.

The story was far less detailed than the headline implied. The only facts were that several books on black magic and Satanism

21

had been found in Gilligan's flat, which was enough for the paper's sensationalist headline. There were no details as to what kind of books these were, whether they were serious studies of the occult or the common or garden paperbacks that could be found in any branch of Waterstones or Smiths.

Laurence kept his eyes on the road ahead when he arrived at Highgate, determined not to look for any hoodies, real or imagined. In a few hours he would be in Brighton with Liz, helping to comfort her over her father. Till then he would do his best to keep the absurdities of the last few days out of his mind.

Back at his flat he wasted no time in tossing some clothes into a travel bag. Though he tried not to look at it like this, he knew that the chance to get away to Brighton for the next few days was just what he needed now, even though it made him feel guilty that it was because of Liz's father. He remembered the last time he met Harry. The old man had been badgering for him and Liz to get their relationship on a more formal setting for months. "Why not go the whole hog and get yourselves engaged?" he asked them. "I'm not getting any younger and I'd like to see my little girl with a ring on her finger, even if a wedding ring's far less likely yet. More's the pity." He'd added that with a rueful, almost roguish grin which Laurence in many ways wished he'd been able to reciprocate with something better than, "Someday perhaps, if Liz is willing."

Now it was too late for the old man to see his "little girl with a ring on her finger".

"Sorry, Harry," he whispered softly. "I'd liked to have done it for you, given the chance."

With a sigh, Laurence headed for the door, bag in one hand and keys in the other, when he saw the man stood at the window.

What happened next seemed to pass in a blur. Laurence remembered the cry – though it could have been a scream – that he uttered as he threw himself towards the door. Though the man's face was impossible to make out against the brightness of the window, he did glimpse the glint of a knife in one hand, its blade reflecting the light as the figure ran towards him, the hood sliding back off his head so that Laurence could see his face at last. He did not need to do more than glimpse him to recognise Paul Gilligan.

Mad Paul Gilligan.

Dead Paul Gilligan.

Paul Gilligan whose body was stored and tagged in a morgue somewhere.

Laurence flung his travel bag at the man in a desperate effort to slow Gilligan down and give himself time to reach the door. But the bag was too light to do more than bounce off Gilligan's chest.

"No!" Laurence shouted; he watched the knife rise in the air, its point aimed at him. "No! God, no!"

It was at that moment that another figure, smaller, less agile, moved across the room, blocking Gilligan's path. At first the other man moved clumsily. Despite this, he threw himself at the killer in a reckless attempt at a body tackle. In that instant of grace, a voice called out at Laurence: *"Go! Go now!"*

Laurence grabbed at the door so hard its lock splintered, then he raced down the stairs so fast he tripped over his own feet, to he burst out onto the street in a tangle of limbs. A dog reared at him, tugging on its lead as its owner, a tall, well-dressed woman, called him a lout. Hands grazed on the paving stones he'd sprawled across, Laurence picked himself up, welcoming the attention of the people around him on the busy street, feeling the safety of their presence, of the cars in the road and the bus by the kerbside, its passengers staring at him as if he was drunk.

Then he remembered the fight in his flat.

The police arrived less than five minutes after he phoned them on his mobile. DC Trubshaw came minutes later. They sealed the flat till an armed response unit had been mobilised to enter the flat armed with guns. The operation lasted less than an hour. Whoever had been inside his flat, though, had gone by the time the first policeman entered it.

Trubshaw was less than sympathetic after he looked around

the flat, unable to find any trace of a fight, apart from the damage that Laurence had done to the door.

Feeling under suspicion of wasting police time, Laurence tried to insist that he hadn't imagined it, but he could see he was getting nowhere except to irritate Trubshaw.

When the police had gone Laurence warily returned to his flat, picked up his travel bag from where it lay by the window, then hurried downstairs. The ground floor lock was still intact and would have to do to protect his flat till he got back. Not that he cared. All he wanted to do was to get out of here and head for Brighton. He was not even sure if he ever wanted to return here again.

*

It was over two hours by the time he reached Brighton and found a taxi to take him to the hospital to meet Liz and her sister. Whatever he expected to see when he got there, though, he was not prepared for the distress they were in – or the large numbers of police.

"What's happened?" he asked as Liz ran to him, her face blotched with tears. "What's wrong?"

She hugged him, unable to speak. It was a uniformed policewoman who gave him the facts, such as they were – of how, after he had died, it was found that Liz's father had been stabbed in the chest and that someone had managed to cut off one of the old man's thumbs.

It was then that Laurence realised he recognised the voice that had shouted to him in the flat, as he hugged onto Liz even harder.

A BOTTLE OF SPIRITS

Phyllis Harker had always wanted to be a clairvoyant, and yet, despite her every strain and effort, failure always faced her in the end. It was because of this that it came as a profound shock when, what to all appearances was one of the oldest and least sure tricks of the trade, suddenly brought her success. In one last fit of desperation she sat at the writing desk by her open window, a pen held loose between her fingers as the books she had read had told her. She held her breath a moment, then breathed slow and calmly to force the tension from her bones. With a jerk the pen moved. Page after page was filled with what it wrote, and in a style which skilled graphologists will swear bears no resemblance at all to that of Phyllis Harker.

This is what it said:

"My name is Rob. I had no other, nor know of ever having any other. Through childhood I lived in a home of sorts. But I can't 'member much of it now. When I were thirteen, I ran away and never went back. My past I cut off with a wall of repugnance and thought only of the present and all that I met, experienced and saw from then on.

"But the future seemed to promise as little as that which I swore to forget had brought, and at first it seemed my luckiest day when I saw Sebastian Preskett.

"He worked a mind reading act in the Grand Theatre, Clayborn-by-the-Sea. At the time I worked behind the curtains, pushing off old props and pushing on new ones for the next act. That wasn't all, but it'll do for starters. In between I sometimes managed to watch a little of what was happening on stage from the wings.

"Preskett was like a Messiah to me. How he did his tricks I felt sure I could never understand. I'd never gone in for religion. My life had given me little enough to have any gratitude in my Divine Creator, and the nearest I'd ever come to praying was to

25

swear once or twice that if He did exist, I'd tear out his guts and spit on 'em. But Preskett, though, Preskett was as near as I could imagine to a God. An old times God, like they used to have before they nailed Jesus to the cross. I knew he used no tricks. With my own eyes I could see this. No assistant on stage, just an old guy he hired to carry his bags and do all his odd jobs when off it. No, no assistant, just himself stood there in his black monkey suit, white tie and tails, and a shiny top hat on a pedestal by him. Besides this there was only one other prop. This was an organ. A wormy old thing made of stained wood and ivory, covered in all sorts of intricate carvings. The pipes were like snakes, with fanged mouths, scale covered and rough. Nothing slimy about them. As slimy as a crocodile but as viperous as adders. After introducing himself with the usual ham oration he would seat himself at the organ and gaze into the bottle fixed above its pipes. Perhaps it was this bottle that seemed the queerest thing in the act. It was carved out of crystal and looked heavy, ugly and as old as dry bones, as crumbling stones, and the sands beneath the seas. Inside, it was filled with a pale blue, sparkling liquor that seemed to shift as he played the organ like mounds of agitated amoebas, rising and falling all the time. Then, when he'd got it all stormy, and the stage lights played across him so that shadows lengthened into eerie grottoes and the bottle seemed to glow as though full of burning fires or some undersea creature with phosphorescent lobes, he would turn to the audience and ask, in his deep, throaty, whisky-soaked voice, for volunteers to offer something hidden about them for revelation through the powers of his mind. It was as corny as a corncob, but it worked. Some old fool woman out with a bus load of her friends, egged on by them and bottled beer, would stand up holding something hidden by her hands and wait for him to tell us what it was. An old act, yes; but new in that there was no assistant, no words as a secret code to tell him just what she held, only the organ, the bottle and his mind. And, of course, he knew each time just what it was she held, and what the cocky young fellow with his fancy bit held, and what the slumming pip squeak, the char lady, dad with his ice cream-hidden kids, the fat lady, the thin, the smart Alec, and the dumb, he knew what every one of them held. They all tried to fool him with a closely held mitt. And they were all, in the end, defeated.

"The whole summer season I watched this go on from Matinee to closing up time when he'd leave as wordless as he was wordy on stage, the organ taken away in his battered green van, **S. PRESKETT - MIND READER** painted in peeling Gothic letters across each side.

"By the time the season came to a close and the hoardings outside along the sea front were brought inside, the acts packed away, Good Byes called and wages handed out for one last time, I had learnt a lot about Preskett. I knew where he lived: inside a caravan he kept on an empty lot on the outskirts by the ruins of a gutted factory and a sleazy, weed-filled canal. It was a large affair with bill boards around it and a couple of narrow, curtained windows. What it was like inside I had no idea. It looked dark and misbegotten, a creation from this century which seemed too old, far, far too old to be in it. It was paradoxical but true.

"Even so I felt only one wish, and that was to remain with him. But this seemed useless. Preskett didn't need me. The old man who worked for him seemed sufficient for his purposes. Yet, he was old, so very old...

"Slyly, I watched them as they lived in their caravan, moving from town to town to do the night clubs during the winter season, using what money I had managed to save to follow them. Then, one night, I saw the old man leave to go on an errand. By now I knew their routine. It was Monday, the start of a new week. At nine thirty that night, as a black drizzle fell from a sky as dark as burnt wood, I saw him making his tottering way to the nearest off license. To get there he had to pass an alley between a closed down fish and chip shop and a terraced tenement. As he passed, I pounced. His bald head glittered in the distant lamplight. There was a thud. And a dull red line clawed its way across his skull as his glasses shattered on the ground.

"The next few days I spent in a nearby town slouching in pubs while I waited and read through the local papers. Sure enough that next Friday I saw an ad':

ODD JOB MAN WANTED
Willing to travel with entertainer
Lodging provided
Box 11B

"I knew that this was it.

"Catching the next bus, I arrived at the newspaper office on Warner Street, handed in a letter with my address written on it and returned to my lodgings to wait. Two days later I received his reply:

"Dear Mr. Rob,

"I read with interest your application for the job I advertised in the paper and would ask if you would be so kind as to meet me in the Railway Hotel near the station in order to reach a satisfactory arrangement. I would suggest 2 p.m.

"Yours sincerely,

"Sebastian Preskett."

"The next day I left early and arrived there in good time for our meeting. But, like me, he had come early as well and was already there. Quickly I ordered myself a Guinness and went over to him.

""Mr Preskett?" I asked, knowing full well who he was. "My name is Rob." I touched my cap and took the seat opposite. His face was sallow, thin and deeply lined like that of a statue carved from the bare rock of a mountain, worn deep where rain had sluiced down as waterfalls and fissured where ice had expanded and probed with its destructive fingers. His hair was a black skull cap, his clothes the cast-off remnants of gentility. Large hands that seemed like bones thick with over full veins and arteries beneath a thin veil of skin twitched round a glass of whisky.

"He smiled as though it hurt to do so. "Have I seen you before?" His voice was round and enveloped me like a balloon of sound.

"Truth, I felt, would be best, and I said that he had. "At Clayborn," I said. "I was a stage hand there for t' summer season."

"Slowly he looked me over from head to foot. "What a coincidence," he said finally.

""I admired your act very much, Mr Preskett," I interjected.

"He tilted his head benignly.

"I finished my Guinness and waited.

""You did not know it was I who was offering the job? Clayborn is a long way from here and there are many towns in between." His eyes regarded me for a moment with undisguised suspicion - yet distantly, as if I was hardly worth it.

""No, Mr Preskett," I lied - somewhat nervously I might add. "It must've been luck, pure luck. But I do need that job."

""So you do. Very well." He drew himself up, released the glass and stood, drawing back from the table. "Very well, I'll hire you. You can come with me now before collecting your things and I'll show you what your job entails. I hope it won't prove adverse to what you desire."

"My lodging in the caravan was a small cubby hole opposite the door and to one side of an inner door in a partition dividing this section of the caravan from his personal rooms. It was large, like the back of a removal truck, fitted out for living in. The colours inside were dull or else faded, with lengths of damp paint hanging from the walls like flayed skin. Oil lamps simmered with black tails whipping up at the ceiling, widening already large stains. My bed was a bundle of moth-eaten blankets on a bug-ridden mattress rolled across the floor. A calendar hung above my head and the edge of a paraffin heater stood by my feet so I'd be warm in the winter. After my first day of work for Sebastian Preskett I settled down late that night satisfied and very, very, very tired.

"The next week we moved on to Preston, and from there, the week after, to Chorley. Accrington followed, and Burnley followed that, and Colne followed both. Onwards we travelled as snow fell fat on the trees and the sky grew as grey as bad teeth. Winds whistled at night as if ghosts filled the wheels beneath the old caravan, only the red glow of the heater staving off complete darkness as I snuggled up, ready for sleep.

"During the days I worked - and worked hard. Off stage Preskett may have been a man of few words, but this economy meant only a more crisp and sharp command, and my jobs were many and varied: making coffee, stewing beef, darning socks, carrying props and whatever else needed carrying, changing wheels, hitching the caravan, cleaning it and buying everything from tooth paste to whisky. The awe I felt for him did not lessen. The mystery, the enigma that held me in its fascinating clasp was still there. Familiarity - if our relationship could be described as familiar - bred no contempt. How he did his act I still did not know. He never rehearsed nor made any arrangements with folk to appear in the audience as his 'volunteers'. Nothing was fixed. It was as legitimate as the Royal Mint, as miraculous as the raising of Lazarus, the curing of the lepers or the parting of the Red Sea. Impossible, I knew, outrageously so, yet incontrovertibly true. How no one saw this or the implications in it I do not know. I'm no genius. Yet I DID SEE. Why didn't anyone else? Or are people so used to being tricked, they expect and accept it? And feel snug in their prosy lack of awareness, safe behind a firm belief in 'It's all done with mirrors' or 'It's clever but it's fixed' or a million and one tricks they suspect but can't pin point, never realising for one instant that it was not cardboard fakery at all.

"But though I realised this, that he did, somehow, by some occult means, either read people's minds or see behind their hands, just how it was done I did not know. Why I wanted to I'm not really sure. Curiosity? The desire to copy him in some way, emulating his act? Or to steal his secret and make a lot of money selling it? One or all or none of these reasons? Whichever no longer matters. What made me, made me, and pry I soon did. Before the first month had passed, I'd been over every inch of the caravan, searching for anything that might even hint how he did it. But nothing did. Humdrum, that is all I can say about what I found inside his rooms. A few dirty books were all I found outside the usual, if even they're outside the 'usual'. Only one thing remained, a thing that had been gnawing at me for some time: the organ locked inside the van. Never was his act carried out without it. No effect really warranted it, though. Its weirdly deep tones and baleful tunes served only as well as a good band, and most places had these. Yet he never made do with them. Always the organ and its phosphorescent bottle jutting out from its pipes.

"My first chance to get a look at it came one night after an unusually strenuous day when Preskett retired early, exhausted. Tired as well, only the knowledge that such opportunities were rare gave me the energy to creep out of the caravan and hide in the shadows between it and the van, a length of wire in my hand. My experiences earlier in life during a time I would rather forget, when impatience and greed led me into petty theft, had left me well prepared for what followed, and soon I was peering into the van, a pocket torch throwing its beam across baroque gargoyles and figurines startled into immobility. Angelic wings and Mephistophelian horns glimmered like sculptures of molten gold blackened by age with outreaching claws and hillocks of scales, flared nostrils and mouths scattered in a nightmarish jungle of pandemonic atrocities, fountains of solidified smoke coiling up from behind as though Hell itself had been seen and reproduced in the hard, fine grained wood and ivory by a sculptor of demonic genius. The pipes seemed to sway as I moved the torch nearer like cobras mesmerised by a snake charmer's flute. I crouched over it, my head touching the roof as I looked closely at the bottle. Like an iceberg, most of it I knew must be beneath the surface, only the deeply carved chest and its neck sticking out. The blue radiance lay still now, glowing dimly as I imagine glow-worms glimmer whilst asleep. Did this organ help him in some way, like a machine? Some kind of television, perhaps? Though if it was, he was wasting his time as a magician. He could make a fortune out of it. No camera, no external devices visible to anyone. But no, I knew I was fooling myself. This was no kind of television. Though it could be connected in some way with telepathy. Did it let him read minds? I shuddered at the thought. After all, if it did, he could one day, couldn't he, discover how I'd got the job, and why? No, it was too dangerous, I decided, feeling a wave of panic rush over me. Either I found out what it was or else I put it out of action and got away from him as fast as I could. He was too much of a potential threat to me. I felt frightened, God-awful frightened suddenly, and I shook till I felt my bones would jar loose.

"It was that bottle, I felt sure, gave the organ its peculiar powers. Ruthlessly I grasped the panelling along the front and pulled until, with a rending of wood, a precipice of demons and hydras came free and I could see what lay hidden beneath.

"Only the bottle stood there, widening out into a globe of glass like the belly of a Buddha. Clawed lions' feet held it on a wooden rest above the pipes and lines of tubes below. Inside glowed the blue liquor. Perhaps it was this that gave Preskett his powers? By now I had given up most of my hopes of finding out how it worked, or why. All I could do was destroy it so that he couldn't find out about me.

"On top of the bottle was a bulbous glass stopper shaped like a dragon's head, with claws hung round its rim. Holding it tightly, I turned it one way then another. It was so tight that it seemed at first to be joined to the bottle with every atom of its being. Slowly, though, I felt it start to work loose as I prised it further and further. There was a crack and a high, shrieking hiss.

"The world spun with iridescent serpents of blues upon blues. I heard a door slam shut as I tottered across the van, azure flames and streamers and comets screaming round and round, going further outwards and then further till they reached the rust smeared sides of the van. And still they went outwards into the van's walls and then beyond them, as though they were only shadows of reality to these madly racing whips. Terror seized me and, trembling, I scrambled round to get out. As I reached for the door handle behind me it moved out of my reach and Preskett thrust his face up to mine.

""What the 'ell are you doing?" Blood pressure made his temples pulse and his eyes explode with veins. "What 'ave you done?" He pushed me aside and my head struck something hard behind me as he glared at the organ. The blue spirals shivered ever wider, disappearing in their gyrations like smoke streams in a gale. Somewhere something seemed to laugh.

"Preskett grabbed and shook me by the throat. "You fool. Look what you've done. Look what you've done!"

""I'm sorry, Mr Preskett, sir," I stammered. "But it wasn't me. Honest, it wasn't. I 'eard someone. Jus' now. An' I came out to look. But there were too many and they pushed me away."

""Heard? What did you hear?" He tightened his grip on my jacket and pressed me against the van's wall as if to squeeze talk out of me.

""Some men. There were four o' them. They grabbed the bottle an' one o' them said: "Let's tek it, it's prob'ly valuable." An' then I rushed 'em."

""You're lying." Preskett's mouth overspilled with spittle. "You're lying. There were no men here. I didn't hear them, and I was not asleep. But I did hear you."

"Through my confusion and fear I stammered out apologies. "It were an accident," I said, cringing against the wall.

""An accident, eh?" He cocked his head on one side. "An accident of prying!"

""I'll make it up to you. Honest I will."

""Make it up? And do you think you can? Do you really think you can? Do you swear it? Will you swear to it?"

"I gibbered out: "Yes."

""Then swear, come on swear: I promise on my immortal soul..."

""I promise on my immortal soul."

""...to repair the damage that I caused..."

""To repair the damage that I caused."

""...even should it cost me my very life..."

"Through the silence that followed only a deep, reverberant booming beneath my ribs remained.

""...even should IT COST ME MY VERY LIFE!"

"I acquiesced.

"No sooner had the words been formed than he cried out in triumph and leapt back, hurling me at the ground. Overbalanced, I had time and initiative only to scream out in terror before a blind, eternal flash of agony sprang up from my snapping neck and my body convulsed into a crumpled heap on the ground.

"But now I know. I know what gave (or seemed to give) Preskett his mind reading powers. But the music grows louder and I haven't much time. It's calling to me, calling to me with its weirdly deep tones and baleful tunes, and I can't resist.

"The blue souls of the dead - Oh, God help me - The blue souls of the dead and damned on earth - It's a trap, a Hellish trap - I shan't become his slave - Legends of genii, distorted by age, but true, oh so true - True - The bottle - Oh God - Help me, please help.

"HELP ME... HELP.

"Oh the bottle... oh the spirits that it held in servitude and purgatorial damnation...

"I can't resist anymore.

"Oh please help, hel...

"The bottle - the music, it grows louder.

"Hel... help, HELP ME... PLEASE - the music - the music - calling...

"calling... CALLING

"break the bottle Preskett, SEBASTIAN PRESKETT

"god! too much pain

"Preskett at night clubs easy to find

"but break the bottle

"i don't want to be his slave

"please help help before *THE PAIN*

"music calling calling call call..."

NO SENSE IN BEING HUNGRY, SHE THOUGHT

Rain dripped past the bricks of the tenement, falling with leaden splashes in the dark backyard around Moorby's feet. Slippery underfoot, with a slimy mixture of garbage and mould, Moorby remained still, his chest heaving as his overtaxed lungs tried to suck more oxygen in to make up for what they'd used in his panic-stricken race down back streets and alleys minutes before, police car beacons shredding the darkness - a nightmare disco gone horribly wrong. He thought he'd lost them. He hoped he'd lost them, as he stared down the yard to the black bulk of the wall at the end. He'd closed the solid wooden gate behind him, piling a heap of loose bricks against it to give the impression to anyone outside it was securely bolted, though the bolt itself was too thick with rust to move.

Soaked to the skin, his dark track suit clung to Moorby's overweight body as he shivered, his face almost blue with cold. If there had been any light in the yard, the dense archipelagos of acne on his cheeks and over his chin would have stood out like splashes of Day-Glo paint as anger burned inside him, competing with his fear of being caught. As if it was a crime - a *real* crime - to do what he'd done to the bitches, he thought. They'd asked for it. Begged for it. For all their hypocritical screams. They'd asked for it all right. If they hadn't, why did they tempt him, flaunting their sex, the filthy whores? The filthy, stinking...

Car tyres crunched along the alleyway. They made Moorby tense, his outrage stilled as panic jammed all but a few terror-filled circuits in his brain. For minutes that seemed to stretch into hours, he barely dared to breathe as he listened with almost painful intensity to the discordant sounds of the police radio crackling inside the car. He heard its door open and someone step out to walk down the alley with slow, careful steps. A flashlight beamed beneath the gate, but it failed to reach Moorby's feet, blocked by clumps of sodden grass between the paving stones inside the yard.

Seeing nothing suspicious, the policeman slowly - perhaps reluctantly - returned to his car.

Moorby's chest slumped in relief when the car began to drive away, the rain quickly drowning the sound of its engine as it went down the alley.

The bitch!

He'd almost had her. If she hadn't pulled a canister of hair spray out of her coat pocket and caught him with a blast of it straight in one eye at point blank range, she'd have stood no chance. Once he'd dragged her into the park beyond the bushes, he'd have fucked her senseless on the grass.

Hatred seethed through Moorby's brain as he thought about what should have happened next.

The worst of it was, as she ran down the road away from the park, screaming her head off, a police car was driving the opposite way. If it hadn't, he'd have had time to drag her back, one eye screwed in agony or not. He'd have managed it somehow, he knew. Then she'd have suffered,

She'd have suffered all right...

Moorby clenched his fleshy, cold, blue fists as he let the emotion swell through his body.

Stiff with tension, Moorby stared into the darkness, allowing his frustration to run unchecked. He'd have to find someone tonight. Whatever the risks, he had to do it. He felt as if he would explode if he didn't.

Moorby picked his way between the garbage dumped in the yard, back towards the gate, when he heard a noise in the house behind him. Surprised, he glanced up as a light flashed on behind the bedroom window, illuminating the tattered, pale green curtains drawn across it. Up until now he had automatically assumed the house was empty. The downstairs windows had been boarded up, and there was a distinctive smell of decay in the small backyard; all the hallmarks of a derelict house. Were there squatters, perhaps? His brows bristled above his nose as he tried to think it through.

The curtains twitched open and a face peered out through the gap.

Quickly, Moorby backed against the kitchen wall. His lips curled as he glimpsed a girl's face peep between the curtains. She was young, perhaps seventeen. Maybe less. Weak-looking chin, pale hair, pallid cheeks. Couldn't have weighed much more than six stones, he thought, sizing her up. Perhaps not even that.

A featherweight.

Prey.

Moorby liked that thought. It added an aura of glamour to what he was doing.

Prey for the hunter, his mind went on... for the predator!

The local press, in between sensational stories about a banned National Front march in Burnley and UFO sightings in Rossendale, had had space to dub him the Night Hawk Rapist, named after the black balaclava he wore when he attacked his victims, NIGHT HAWK stitched across its forehead - though he'd heard himself described in his local pub less flatteringly as the "fuckin' Shite 'Awk" by men incensed at the fear the rapist had created in the area. There had even been mounted police patrols till late at night along certain roads to help quell fears amongst local residents, ensuring that women could at least venture out in some sort of safety by themselves on the main thoroughfares. But not, Moorby thought, with some satisfaction, not when they left them.

His thick fingers, bulging with fat, tingled with anticipation.

He stared at the bedroom window. If the girl was in there alone...

Moorby listened intently. If she spoke to someone inside the room, he'd know he was wasting his time. But if she didn't, if she really was alone up there... If she was...!

Her eyes, dim shapes in her shadowy face, moved from side to side as if she was trying to see through the darkness below.

37

For a few seconds more she stared through the window, then drew back again, closed the curtains behind her and silently retreated to her bed... to her lonely, unshaped bed, he thought, a coppery taste lining his mouth.

Tensely, he licked his lips, dried as adrenaline surged into his groin.

He'd never done it inside someone's house before. His favourite spots had always been parks, where there were scores of places in which to hide - and as many routes for escape.

He had good memories of parks, with their dark woodlands of elms and alders, their dense patches of rhododendrons, and their rolling hills and inter-linking paths.

Perhaps now, as winter began to draw in, it was time to branch out. Instead of a few snatched moments on cold, rain-soaked grass, hidden between shrubs, he could satiate himself in the comfort of someone's room... in someone's bed.

Moorby crept towards the kitchen door. Experimentally, he pressed his shoulder against it, then slowly, carefully exerted more pressure.

The door began to give at once.

There was a creak of wood splintering behind it. Rotten.

He pushed even harder. Reaching through the gap he'd forced, he felt the Yale lock behind it, hanging useless, all but one of its screws torn from the wood. Only the fact that the door had jammed against the uneven floor inside prevented him from opening it wider. But the two-foot gap was wide enough, even for Moorby's seventeen stones.

He squeezed into the unlit kitchen and felt his way along the damp surface of its worktop towards the door into the rest of the house.

His fingers touched the handle of a knife - a bread knife, left on the worktop surrounded by crumbs. But his own knife was better; hidden inside his track suit; sheathed at his waist. Its steel blade was nine inches long, with a razor-sharp edge. He could feel its reassuring weight against his leg. He reached into his pocket, down through the hole he'd cut to reach it. He could get a hard on just looking at that knife, unsheathed. Even if there was someone here besides the girl, there was always this. Few men would try to bar his way once they saw the knife. He wouldn't, he knew.

He smiled. Somehow, he didn't expect he'd need it tonight.

Down a passageway as dark as a mine shaft, he felt his way along the wall into an empty room at the front of the house, its dim floorboards faintly registering on his optic nerves from what little light managed to scrape between the boards nailed across the window. Ahead of him now, the pane of a window above the front door showed through the vestibule door, itself made of glass, coated in dust. He touched it as he made his way past, feeling the gritty surface beneath his fingers. Up the dark staircase that faced the door, one step at a time, placing his feet as near as he could to the edge of the steps. Up past the bend halfway up the stairs. Up towards the landing through wisps of cobwebs hung from the ceiling, his breath so hushed it hurt his chest.

Feet to the edge of the skirting board to ease the strain on the floorboards and stop them creaking, he headed along the landing. A musty smell of decay filled the air. Of wet plaster. Of mould.

Unsure of himself suddenly as he looked down the landing towards the stairs, he felt for his knife. He missed the open spaces of Corporation Park, with its ease of escape. It seemed as if the further he went into the house, the more claustrophobic it felt. Less confident now, he wondered if he had been justified in being certain a few minutes ago that the other rooms upstairs were empty. Hesitantly, he headed towards the bedroom at the front. Its door stood ajar. Pushing it lightly, it swung open. In the afterglow from the lamp post outside he was relieved to see its bare floorboards were bare apart from scattered newspapers and a pile of junk in a cardboard box by the window. Vaguely, he could make out scrawled, paint-sprayed graffiti on the walls, whose lengths of floral wallpaper were beginning to unpeel from the damp plaster. Dark bulges, like huge pupae, hung from the dim expanse of the ceiling, which Moorby took for large masses of fungus.

Satisfied there was no one in the room, Moorby tried the door across the landing. The bathroom stank of an unflushed toilet, heavy with whatever had been dumped into it. Wood lice crawled across twilit walls, as if the patterned wallpaper had begun to move.

This had to be a squat, Moorby thought, its condition so bad it had finally been abandoned by everyone except the girl. More confident now, Moorby headed towards the bedroom at the back. Time for caution was almost over now, he thought, feeling an anticipatory stirring inside his pants as he pulled the balaclava out of his pocket and drew it over his head. He pulled out his knife, knowing the sight of it would quickly quieten the girl. His left hand pressed on the door handle as he pushed it open, striding through.

The girl lay on an tangle of blankets on top of a mattress on the floor, in a room bare of anything apart from a few large plastic bags. She stirred as he stepped towards her. Moorby grinned. The Night Hawk had found his prey at last.

"Hey, wake up! Lover boy's here!" he whispered, relishing the callous harshness of his humour. He grasped the edge of the blankets and tugged them from her.

The girl, looking frail in the gloom, reached for the lazy switch above her head, but Moorby moved towards her too fast. One hand gagged her mouth as his weight overpoweringly bore down on her, relentlessly forcing her back onto the mattress, his other hand holding the knife in front of her eyes.

"One sound and I'll cut you," he said. "I mean it. I'll cut you bad."

He felt her body grow stiff beneath him as he pulled at her clothes, his sensations taking over from rational thought in the heat of the moment. More than ever before he felt himself drawn into a dreamlike delirium, within which he was barely aware of what he was doing. They rolled on the mattress, her weakness so obvious he threw aside his knife. One moment he held her down on top of him. The next they rolled over, and he pressed himself on top of her, spreading her beneath him.

Pleasure and pain were entangled in a whirlpool that swirled through his head.

Moorby grunted as pleasure passed, and a dull pain started his groin.

He snarled, aware that something he had never experienced before was happening to him. He tried to stand up, but his arms weren't free.

"What is it?" He opened his eyes, but the room was too dark. Something held his arms. Panicking, he tried to tug himself free.

Then he felt the knife. His knife, was it? It jabbed him, cutting through clothes and flesh with equal ease. This couldn't be happening to him, he thought, as the blade stabbed into his shoulder. He pulled one arm free, and felt his fingers cut as the blade sliced through them, heading for his chest. It hit him so hard it punched the air from his lungs. "Hey, stop it!" he wanted to say to whoever was attacking him. Blood bubbled from his lips, tasting salty in his mouth as it rose like phlegm - like pints of phlegm - in his throat.

As if his attacker was excited by the blood, the knife flashed frenziedly back and forth. Again and again. Moorby felt the agonising pain of its blade stabbing deep into his arms and legs, then into his body. Blood slicked the floor, making his feet skid as he tried to step back away from the bed. He slipped onto the mattress. It felt like a sponge, wet with blood. His blood!

The knife moved again. It was heading for his face. He tried to duck, but its point pinned the "T" of the emblem on his balaclava onto his forehead. "No!" His voice cried in despair as the blade bore down again. "No! Please!" Till the bone began to give and the blade slid home... slid deep into his brain.

*

In the damp room the girl rose from the mattress, glancing at the thing that was laid on the floor. As sunlight shone between

41

the curtains, she looked at it, frowning, puzzled why the man had come to her. She gazed at the body, her frown fading. It was time to dress, she told herself as she heard the others in the room moving down towards the floor. At least they'd been able to rest while she kept watch.

She looked at her arms. Her skin began to move, its textured folds like wet cloth.

Beige today, she told herself, and her skin changed colour.

And wool. A woollen jumper to keep me warm. That would be best. No sense in looking odd in weather like this.

No sense in looking odd at all. She reached out, feeling the lumps of blood on the body beside her. No sense in being hungry, either, she thought, as mouths opened up on the tips of her fingers. Small mouths, ready to suck.

Beneath Moorby's head a bloodstained copy of the local newspaper was spread across the floor. Below its main headline:

HUNT FOR RAPIST INTENSIFIES

a second, smaller headline read:

MORE UFO SIGHTINGS CLAIMED

NOW AND FOREVER MORE

The little village looked somehow frail and insubstantial in the drizzle against the pale grey glow from the sea, as if the spray from the waves that broke against the jagged rocks had momentarily invoked a mirage between the wind-swept hills on either side. The flaking, whitewashed walls of the clustered houses, that stretched around the bay in row after row up the lower slopes of the hills, seemed, if anything, to accentuate this impression of unreality. Daniels shivered, with a feeling of depression, as he stepped with his wife, Julie, down the empty path from the cliffs, his broad face reddened by the winds that lashed into them, tinged with salt. Julie tightened her hand about his as the village came into sight.

"Only one more day," Daniels said in reply to her unvoiced remark. "Then we can go on to St. Auban. I promise. You'll like it much better there, even in weather like this."

When they booked their stay here earlier in the year, neither of them had expected to find this 'unspoiled' village on the Cornish coast to be quite as dispiriting as this. It was not so much the weather, though, they knew, even if this was what they had somehow or other come around to blaming so far since their arrival, nor was it the general quietness of the place, since this was why they had chosen to come here originally. Julie knew that her husband needed a break after all the long hours he'd been putting into work recently. They'd been married for just over two years now and had moved several months ago into their first proper home, after living in a flat above a row of shops in Wolverhampton. After much discussion they had decided that this was what they needed to do if they were to start a family - something which now, to her great relief, they had decided to do. She smiled to herself as she thought of her brother, Arthur. He'd been married just a year longer than them and already he and Lorraine had a two-year-old daughter. She'd enjoyed being the little girl's aunt, but that wasn't enough. She wanted - in fact, she *needed* - a baby of her own.

Julie caught sight of the Broken Mast, where they had a first-floor room. She wondered whether it was the atmosphere of that place that upset them so much, as flecks of spray from the bordering quay scattered across the smooth-worn cobbles about their feet as they strolled along the street towards it. The small-paned windows of the Broken Mast gleamed in the pallid light like deep black glossy stones set within its plaster walls. Daniels squared his shoulders as they walked towards it, almost as if he was preparing himself for a distasteful ordeal.

"Let's not go in just yet," Julie suggested suddenly, tugging his arm.

"Why ever not?" Daniels asked in surprise. He was cold already from their walk along the path that meandered across the cliffs, and his trousers were soaked. "Where else can we go in this place?"

A seagull screamed across the sky, gliding with its great white wings outstretched against the buffeting winds beyond the swaybacked roofs of the houses opposite. Their empty windows mirrored the empty lifelessness of the street.

"We could always have a look at the church," Julie suggested hopefully, looking up the street away from the sea to where an unimpressive, stone-built spire rose bluntly above the trees. "We haven't been yet," she continued, "and it does look old. There might be something of interest for us to look at, I suppose. Besides," she said, wrinkling her nose at the inn, "anywhere would be better than that miserable hole."

Quietly they made their way through the village, arm in arm. The sound of the sea died away behind them to a subdued hush as they rounded a bend in the street and started to climb the steep incline from the bay. The church rose almost furtively before them, its stout walls all but hidden behind a grove of elms, whose knotted roots disrupted the even surface of the ancient burial ground.

Julie smiled hopefully as they pushed open the wrought iron

gate in the surrounding wall, her face tense against the cold. Daniels knew that she would be better off in the inn, where at least she could get warm. It was senseless trailing here on a day like this. But, he supposed, as he looked around at the lichened and unreadable headstones, leaning at odd angles all about them, it was too late to turn back now.

"It looks quite old," Julie said as she looked up at one of the stained-glass windows, in which a bearded saint was depicted frowning at a snake about his feet.

"And neglected," he added heavily, pointing out a broken hole in one of the windows. "The wind probably howls like a pack of wolves through a hole like that."

"It certainly doesn't say much for whoever's supposed to look after it, I suppose," Julie admitted as they peered through the porch into the gloomy interior of the church. A cobweb, silvered with drops of rain, was stretched across one of the upper corners of the arched doorway.

"Shall we go in?" Julie asked, following his gaze across the heavy door.

"We might as well, now we're here," he replied unenthusiastically.

Although the damp mustiness of the air inside the church was unpleasant, Daniels was surprised at how different the atmosphere seemed, almost as if they had somehow stepped out of a clinging fog of depression and were surrounded by clean air at last, which was strangely paradoxical, since the air was certainly no fresher than outside - very much the opposite, in fact - yet, when he looked across at his wife beside him, he could see that this change had obviously been felt by her as well, in the way in which the lines of tension about her frail, sometimes elfin face were visibly beginning to relax as she gazed about herself at the dark interior of the church, her gloved hands gliding appreciatively across the polished wood of the fine old carvings that stood out along the rows of pews.

Their footsteps echoed through the church as they walked down the nave. Daniels' first impressions of neglect were quickly confirmed by the swathes of dust blown into drifts about the paved floor, whilst folds upon folds of grey cobwebs were gathered like discarded blankets between the pews and about the windows. Pointing these out, Daniels said:

"This place hasn't been used for months, perhaps years. The font's full of filth and as dry as a bone, the few cushions still left hanging behind the pews look as if they're ready to fall apart with decay, while the whole place stinks of neglect." He shuddered with revulsion.

Julie stared up at the clotted shadows between the web-draped beams that spanned the ceiling.

"But it's the only church here. How could it have possibly been allowed to fall into disuse like this? It doesn't make sense."

"I don't know. It baffles me as well, sweetheart. But look at it. In another couple of years it'll be too unsafe for anyone to come in and look round it, if it isn't unsafe already." He shrugged. "It's odd, I'll admit it. Small communities like this usually stick to their churches through thick and thin. Or so it's *usually* supposed. Even if there might've been some turning away from the church in recent years, I wouldn't have expected it to be as total as this. Yet, from the look of this place, that's what must have happened here."

Where a cross should have stood on the altar, there was a heap of dried leaves. The altar cloth was stained with blotches of what looked like mildew and had been tugged violently to one side.

"You'd think someone ransacked the place at some time," Daniels said. He shook his head, puzzled, as he felt at the altar cloth. "Damp," he remarked, letting it go and rubbing his fingers clean on the sides of his coat.

"We surely can't have missed seeing another church in a village as small as this," Julie said.

"Unless they're going to one in the next town."

"But St. Auban's too far away. I can't imagine them travelling all that way."

Beginning to bore of the subject, Daniels wished now that he had insisted straight away on returning to the inn instead of trailing out here. He turned his back on the altar and said:

"We could speculate uselessly for hours and get no nearer the truth. We'd be better off returning to the Broken Mast now while it's dry. With any luck we can have insulated ourselves against the locals with a rose-tinted alcoholic haze before they start rolling in later on."

*

As they returned into the village, Daniels noticed one of the local fishermen, sat with his back to them by the quay, where he stared with a kind of fixed solemnity across the lines of moored fishing boats that swayed slowly in the waves washing against them. His rounded shoulders and sunken head made the old man looked like a large, half-filled sack, over which someone had carelessly thrown an oilskin coat and a dirty, old, woollen cap. Salt-stiffened strands of dank, white hair stuck out from beneath his cap in forlorn spikes. For a moment, as they approached him across the wet cobblestones, he was motionless, deep in thought. Then, slowly, hearing their footsteps, he turned and watched them draw towards him. His thick lips sagged into a scowl, a trickle of saliva appearing in one corner, before he wiped it away with the back of his calloused hand.

"Good evening," Daniels said, as they paused for a moment, breathing in the salty air from the sea as it blew in their faces.

The man grunted something in reply, his eyes passing smugly from Daniels to his wife. Daniels felt Julie's hand tighten about his.

"It's about time this weather started to improve a bit," Daniels went on conversationally, almost gabbling, though he could not have explained why he was making the effort to arouse something like a normal human response from the man. He knew that he might just as well have left him alone for all the good it would do. They had tried on more occasions than they cared to remember in the past few days to start some sort of conversation with one of the villagers. Apart from Marsh, the far from loquacious landlord of the Broken Mast, they had never had anything more than a partial and misleading success. "I notice none of the boats have been out today. I expect you'll be waiting for the weather to improve so you can get in some more fishing."

The man shrugged carelessly, turning away. A smell, like that from an uncleaned stable, seeped into the air. It was a smell which they had begun to grow used to when near the villagers who, all of them, possessed it to some degree or another. Although they had initially found it repulsive, they had begun, after the first couple of days, to find it just about bearable. Now, though, after the musty but somehow cleaner air of the church, it seemed even worse than before, and Daniels had to grit his teeth against the nausea it produced. The foul creatures probably never even washed, he thought with indignant disgust, a disgust intensified by the careless ease with which the man deliberately ignored them.

"Come on," Daniels said thickly, "we'll get back to the inn. I could do with a strong drink to wash away some of the stench of this place."

Julie's face paled apprehensively as they continued on their way down the street past the old cottages, with their small windows and salt-stained walls. In his anger Daniels had spoken intentionally loudly so that the ignorant old fisherman would hear him. His jaw tightened aggressively, and Julie could tell that his patience with the village and its inhabitants was coming to an end.

"Only one more day, sweetheart," she reminded him as they approached the Broken Mast, its unvarnished, almost featureless sign swinging back and forth in the gusts of wind with a grating, yet melancholy squeak.

"One more day!" he grunted, as he pushed open the door into the inn. "And one more night too!"

*

48

Later that evening, after they had eaten their dinner and retired into the twilit, oak-filled bar for a drink, Daniels said:

"I suppose I shouldn't have lost my temper with that old bastard on our way back from the church."

Circling her hands about a glass of gin and tonic, Julie lowered her head. "He asked for it," she said quietly. "They've no right to be so rude all the time. They act as if anyone from outside their own squalid, little village was somehow subhuman."

Daniels chuckled.

"And yet, if there was ever a group of people I could have possibly had the gall to call subhuman, it would be the inhabitants of this Godforsaken place." He lowered his voice as several of the locals, the collars of their heavy, rain-soaked coats pulled up about their ears, came in and ordered drinks at the bar. "I've yet to see one of these people," Daniels went on, "who doesn't stink, isn't round-shouldered and doesn't have skin that would look coarse on a pig. I suppose some kind of inbreeding could account for the 'local look'. I'd certainly recognise someone from this place anywhere. There's something about them..."

"Something unhealthy?"

"Like a disease? I suppose so, though I don't think that's it. Not exactly. If, that is, there's anything to be exact about."

"It's your last night 'ere, I b'lieve?" The voice was guttural and loud. Like that of most of the villagers, its accent was not typically Cornish, though Daniels thought that this sounded Northern in some strange way. Surprised at the interest one of the locals should have in them after having been ignored for so long, and at one of them actually opening a conversation for once, Daniels looked round and said:

"That's right. We're off in the morning. We've booked a room in St. Auban for tomorrow night. We'll be leaving on the midday bus."

The man who had spoken was one of the newcomers, tall but stooped, with a long, almost goatish face that looked sick. His dark blue overcoat dripped with rain and there were stains of what looked like slime about his trousers and cuffs. The hand with which he held his beer was heavily discoloured. Worse still, there was a disturbingly gangrenous look to it, especially at the tips of his fingers as he pushed back the glasses perched on his nose, and said:

"You'll be glad to leave 'ere, I s'ppose?"

Wondering whether he was trying to entice him into some kind of criticism of the village, Daniels said, tactfully:

"You can't judge a place properly in weather like this." Having no intention of making an argument with these people, Daniels realised, perhaps for the first time, just how much he had grown to fear them since their arrival here. It was a realisation which he did not particularly like.

The man smiled, though it was poorly done and seemed deliberately false - insultingly so. Daniels felt the blood start to drain from his face, and he knew that he had gone pale. His hand tightened about his drink.

"We carn't 'elp the weather," the man said matter-of-factly, his jaundiced eyes meeting Daniels' in something of a challenge.

"None of us can help the weather," Daniels replied with a shrug of his shoulders.

The other men, silently drinking their pints, watched on, their flaccidly-featured, pale grey faces showing little interest besides that of a thinly concealed contempt. Degenerate bastards, Daniels thought. There seemed an almost natural animosity between themselves and the villagers, as if there was something about both which the other had no choice but to hate. Not for the first time, he wondered what impulse had prompted him to choose a place like Pennerin Bay for a 'relaxing holiday'. Off the beaten track? Unspoiled? Yes, it was both of these things in a sense, though 'unspoiled'? He wondered. Somehow there was something about the village which told him that it was far from unspoiled. In some way it had been, though he could not see what. Not quite.

Their conversation dying in a still, rather embarrassing silence, it was with relief that Daniels diverted his attention back to his wife, laughing quietly, though without much humour, as he took long drinks of his beer.

The night dragged remorselessly by as more and more of the locals stepped in, the subdued humming of their muttered conversations filling the close atmosphere with a disturbing dissidence. No smiles, no jokes, no sudden eruptions of laughter or argument served to break the dull monotony of their talk. And gradually, as the hour grew late and the sky visible through the tiny windows changed from the slate grey of evening to the claustrophobic blackness of night, Daniels found that his nerves were beginning to fray. There seemed to be more of the locals in the bar tonight than usual, and their collective chatter seemed louder, though hardly more distinct, than before.

"That's your eighth pint," Julie chided as he returned with a drink from the bar.

He placed it over-carefully on the beer-slopped table between them, and said:

"It's the only way to wash away their stench." He remembered having said this several times already during the course of the evening.

"Speak quieter," Julie whispered. "They'll hear you."

"So what? Let them know. Why shouldn't they? They do stink, don't they? I'm not exaggerating." He shut his eyes for a moment, and a black void spun vertiginously in front of him. What am I saying? Control yourself, he thought, trying to will himself sober again, though his grip kept slipping. "I'm sorry," he said, pushing his drink away from him. "You're right, it's time I stopped. I've had more than enough already."

"And we've a busy day tomorrow. The bus stops by at twelve, don't forget."

He nodded his head. He wished now that they had brought their car with them, although at the time it had seemed such a good idea to get away from it all and 'learn to use their legs again'. He grunted as he felt a wave of nausea sweep over him.

"I think I'm going to be sick," he muttered. He climbed to his feet and pushed past the empty table next to theirs and staggered towards the Gents. As he lunged through the door into the toilets, he heard someone step in after him.

"You don't look so good." The voice seemed to float in the air about his head, directionless. He said something in reply as his eyes blurred with an overwhelming nausea. He leant over to his left, and his fingers encountered the cold surface of the single enamel sink. Gratefully he drew himself over it and turned on the taps, drops of water splashing back at his face as he sank towards the basin. Almost detachedly, he wondered if he was going to pass out. Everything was going black, a seething maelstrom of darkness that swirled around and around like the water in the sink, sucking him with it down and down and down... He groaned as his stomach heaved; he knew that he was passing out.

*

It seemed, as consciousness passed and the threatening blackness swallowed him up, that he passed into a state which his curiously detached mind regarded as sleep. He felt no surprise at this realisation. He had often enough dreamt of sleeping before, and, doubtless, would do so again. All that concerned him now was the feeling of motion in his legs as if he was walking, though he had no idea why, or where he was going.

Some time passed by in this fashion, when he became aware of a reddish kind of glow ahead of him. Gradually it grew stronger, and he was able to make out more of his surroundings in the encrimsoned gloom: the towering trees that surrounded him with their thick, black trunks and deep morasses of leaves, rustling in the wind - the long-eared blades of grass, still wet with rain in what looked like a clearing - the surrounding blocks of weathered stone that stood like shapeless ghosts, crouching in the long grass - the glimmering red light that revealed itself to be a pile of burning wood. He reached up, as if in a trance, and rubbed his eyes. Something had risen above the surging flames of the bonfire, half hidden in the smoke that billowed from it. He moved forward, feeling someone place their hands on his shoulders and force him down onto his knees. The grass felt wet through his trousers. Wet and cold. Hardly noticing this, he stared, fascinated, at the obscure shape that towered above the flames, untouched by them, his eyes deciphering what looked so much like a great, long, goat-like human head amidst the smoke. Involuntarily, Daniels looked down, away from the face that stared towards him, its yellow eyes looking straight at his with an unwavering gaze. He saw the massive cloven hoofs of the creature, restlessly pounding the earth on either side of the fire.

There was a noise in the air, like a distant chant.

"Ma dheantar aon scriosadh..."

Daniels looked round. A dark procession of cowled figures was advancing from a path amongst the trees, their heads bowed down towards the ground. Slowly, they gathered in huddled lines before the fire.

For a moment Daniels lost consciousness again, and there was a temporary return of the all-encompassing darkness. When it cleared, he was stunned to see that the figures had thrown off their sombre robes, their lumpy, bone-white bodies dyed red in the firelight as they knelt before it, swaying ecstatically from side to side. To his surprise Daniels recognised some of the men and women from the village amongst them. Ugly though they'd seemed when clothed, their nakedness now only served to emphasise their repulsiveness. Their rounded, almost simian shoulders were matted with patches of tangled hair, whilst their stomachs and thighs were almost black with it. Adding even more to their ugliness were other, less healthy blemishes: the running sores and deformities, their cramped, virtually toeless feet, and the coarse, almost pulpy appearance of so much of their pallid skin.

The goat-like head above the fire nodded towards them, and Daniels caught sight of its sulphurously glowing eyes. As if this had been an expected signal, the villagers threw themselves at each other before the bonfire in complete abandon, tugging and groping and thrusting themselves at each others' bodies. It was like some wild, drug-ridden caricature of a Babylonian orgy as they writhed and twisted and groaned, sweat glistening about them as their movements became hectic, as if they were building up to some kind of joint, cumulative climax. Like a mound of swarming, discoloured worms, they rose from the ground in a seething knot of human flesh, coupling together in twos and threes and sometimes more.

Daniels frowned. Till now he had been sure it was only a dream, however disgusting it might seem. As he stared at the hideous cavorting of the villagers, though, he became suddenly aware that what he was watching was real. With each passing second he became increasingly more conscious of his surroundings and of his own physical discomfort as he knelt on the cold, wet grass.

With a cry of horror, he tried to stand up. He shook the hands grasping at his arms off from him and started to turn around. But, before he could see what lay hidden beneath the cowls of the two large men holding him, he saw one of them raise his arm in the air. There was a stick in his fist. It was large and heavy. The next instant he started to cry out as it crashed down at him.

*

"That's a funny kind of lump you've got on the back of your neck," Julie said suddenly, as Daniels carefully shaved himself at the fly-spotted mirror in the bathroom of the Broken Mast, his head aching as if it had been ground paper-thin with emery paper while he slept. "It looks like some kind of rash," she went on, sounding concerned enough for Daniels to crane his neck in the mirror to catch a glimpse of it.

"What kind of rash?" he asked, unable to see anything.

Julie stepped over to him, tying the belt of her dressing gown before reaching out one finger to feel at the rash. She prodded it gingerly, curling her lip.

"I think you'd better get a doctor to have a look at it when we get to St. Auban. It looks sore. Does it hurt?"

Daniels felt at it too. His stomach almost rebelled as he moved his fingers across the lumpish crust of dried skin, perhaps two inches wide, that had formed across the nape of his neck.

"I think I will," he mumbled, his disordered recollections of the nightmare he'd had last night forgotten, as he wondered when or how this had erupted from his flesh. "It doesn't hurt, though. If you hadn't noticed it, I don't think I would have done. Not yet, anyway."

"Well, you'd better have it seen to as soon as we can. Things like that can turn nasty. It looks bad enough already." She hugged his shoulders. "I don't want anything happening to you just because we couldn't be bothered seeing a doctor."

Daniels turned and hugged her back, smiling at her, even though his head still ached with the hangover too many pints in the bar last night had left him with.

Julie combed his hair with her fingers.

"I was worried enough about you last night," she said.

"Last night?" Daniels frowned. "What happened last night?"

Julie laughed carelessly, all the worries she'd had before forgotten now.

"Don't tell me you were so drunk you can't remember where you went? You were away for more than an hour. If the landlord hadn't deigned to tell me you'd slipped outside for a breath of fresh air after being sick in the Gents, I would have been even more worried than I was. Even so, after half an hour of waiting for you in the bar, I was starting to get frantic. I thought you might have stumbled off the quay and got yourself drowned or something..."

"When did I get back?" Daniels asked, his forehead creasing with concern as he tried to remember what had happened. Surely the last thing he did was pass out in the Gents?

"You got back shortly after twelve, your arms over the shoulders of a couple of the locals. A dour-looking pair they were too. They said they found you sleeping near the church, propped up against the cemetery wall. You could have caught your death of cold out there on a night like that," she chided him, realising as she said it that she sounded almost like her mother. Undeterred, she went on: "You didn't even have your coat on. And your clothes were drenched. At some time or another during your rambles about the place you must have wandered off into one of the fields, because your trousers were simply covered in grass seeds. It'll be a wonder if they're not ruined."

Daniels frowned.

"It's like the nightmare I had last night," he told her. "I dreamt I was taken out into one of the fields around here, though..."

"Though what?"

"Though nothing. It was just a dream, that was all. Nothing more. Just a stupid, ridiculous, meaningless dream about some of the locals holding an open-air orgy. There was a bonfire and some kind of presiding demon with a huge goat's head looking on."

"Some nightmare." Julie laughed, her joy at the fact that they would soon be leaving this place obvious as they returned to their cramped, wood-beamed bedroom to finish off their packing. Daniels glanced at the suitcases lying open on their bed, packed full of clothes. He looked past the bed and out through the tiny window that overlooked the woods at the back of the inn, where the hill sloped up from the bay. It was strange how the mere fact that they were leaving here at noon could have buoyed up his wife's spirits, while his own, if anything, were depressed. Yet he knew that he had detested their stay here just as much as she had. Perhaps more so, in fact, since he blamed himself for having picked this God-awful place to start with.

Perhaps it was because she felt well, while he felt as if he was coming down with something. Serve him right if he was, he supposed, after falling asleep, pissed, in the rain. His arms and legs were aching and stiff, and he could feel a griping pain in his chest. As Julie turned her attention to packing the last items in the suitcases, Daniels again passed his fingers across the lump on his neck, hoping that the way he felt hadn't got anything to do with it.

*

After breakfast, served up by Marsh's tight-lipped wife, they decided to go out for a walk. There were another two hours to go before their bus was due, and neither of them felt like spending the time in between cooped up inside the claustrophobic atmosphere of the inn.

"Where shall we go?" Julie asked as they walked down the street a short while later, its cobbles covered in a sheen of water from last night's rain. Patches of blue from between the clouds were reflected in it. "We could always go a last stroll across the cliffs," she suggested, but Daniels shook his head.

"It's still too windy for that," he objected. "Besides, it would take too long."

Aimlessly, they wandered down the street away from the bay, heading up towards the thick woodlands surrounding it. Almost automatically Daniels headed towards one of the rutted lanes that cut meanderingly through the trees, its hedges overgrown with ferns and wild flowers. Although there was no reason for him to choose any particular lane, Daniels had the disturbingly strong impression of being drawn towards this particular one. It was ridiculous, he knew, as was the ache of trepidation in his stomach as he looked along it.

Ridiculous.

Or was it?

He felt a trickle of sweat slither down the side of his face as he gazed about the lane, as if he was looking for something - for some sign, perhaps, that would show he had been here before.

The sky glittered between the overhanging boughs of the trees, the bright green shadows of their canopying leaves giving the lane the appearance of an undersea grotto.

"For the first time this place is actually beginning to look attractive," Julie announced. There was a faint note of regret in her voice, as if she was genuinely disappointed that this should happen just as they were about to leave. Daniels made some murmured comment in reply, too preoccupied in staring round at the trees to take much notice of what she said. What was there about this place, he wondered instead, that he felt so scared of seeing? He was sure that there was something that scared him.

But what?

"Is that smoke up ahead of us?" Julie asked. She pointed to a faint grey blur above the trees, past a bend in the lane.

"I don't know." He could feel his heart pound suddenly. "Probably nothing," he said.

"Nothing?"

"I don't know." He shook his head, his mind too fogged by fears he couldn't even understand to concentrate on what she was talking about. "Some farmers, perhaps, burning rubbish."

"Or your bonfire, the one you dreamt about last night?" she joked, though the joke fell flat on his ears.

He smiled faintly in reply as they continued down the lane. What seemed fleetingly like a large, grey squirrel raced down the side of a beech tree ahead of them, then darted beneath the ferns out of sight. Dispersing through the trees like a dense sea mist blown in from the cliffs, the smoke seemed indifferent to the wind, and unhurried.

They climbed over a turnstile where a fence barred the lane from a narrower, overgrown footpath on the other side; most of its rough, stony surface was hidden beneath tufts of grass.

"Whatever's causing all that smoke can't be all that far ahead of us now," Julie said, sniffing at the air as if this would tell her what she wanted to know.

Daniels glimpsed ahead of them, where the trees opened out, perhaps fifteen or so yards further on, a large, almost circular field. For a moment he thought he could also see something white, like a stone, standing tall in the grass. Suddenly, he knew that he wanted to stop, that he wanted to turn back. It was childish, he knew, and impossible. Julie was far too stubborn -

too self-willed, in fact - to be fobbed off or persuaded by any half-baked excuse he might think up now.

"There's your bonfire," she said, looking round at him with a peculiar mixture of triumph and curiosity on her face.

Daniels, though, had already seen it, even as she spoke. Somehow he had known that he would see it. He had known it all along, at the back of his mind. The smouldering shards of wood piled high in the field crackled noisily to themselves, while here and there a dull red glow glimmered amongst them, like demonic eyes peering gloomily out from the darkness of Hell.

As they left the path and picked their way into the field through the dripping ferns, he saw the odd-looking blocks of stone. They were no longer as startlingly white as they'd seemed in his dream, and he could see that their weather-pitted surfaces were covered with patches of lichens and moss. In their symmetric positioning about the field, equidistant from each other in a rough kind of circle, they looked distinctively like the kind of Druidic temples so frequently depicted in guidebooks.

"Is this *exactly* as you dreamt it?" Julie asked.

"How or why, I don't know, but yes," Daniels answered, as he ploughed his fingers through his hair, looking round himself bewildered - and a little afraid.

"Well, there's one explanation anyway," Julie said. "You *were* here last night. Perhaps you wandered down this lane. And perhaps you really did see something going on here, some rustic celebration perhaps."

"With an orgy?" he asked, incredulous. "And what about the devil-goat? Was that here too?"

Matter-of-factly, Julie said:

"Those you must have dreamed about afterwards. After all, you *were* drunk, dear. And there's the world of difference between this," (and she pointed at the remains of the bonfire) "and a devil-goat."

"I thought this was fantastic enough."

"And the rest is even more fantastic," Julie insisted. "Too fantastic, in fact. And you know it."

"I suppose you're right." Damn it, of course she was right, he told himself irritably. Why was he talking such rubbish? He knew that most of what he thought he saw last night was his own imagination. What if parts of what he seemed to remember did turn out to be true? That didn't automatically mean that everything was, did it?

Daniels looked across at the stones. At one time they might have been cut into some kind of manlike shape, but that must have been a long time ago, and countless rainfalls, winds and snows had worn whatever features the ugly, Henry Moorish things might have had into virtual oblivion.

A log exploded, its overheated juices hissing and spitting like an angry cat.

"Shall we set off back to the inn now?" Julie asked.

The bonfire was slowly caving in. A smoking cinder rolled like a severed head across the wet grass, spluttering.

As they slowly turned to leave, Daniels glimpsed the top of a tousled mop of hair being whipped out of sight beneath the ferns on the far side of the path, followed immediately by the staccato splintering of twigs, which faded hurriedly into the distance.

Exchanging amused glances of perplexity, they returned to the lane past the turnstile. Something cracked in the branches overhead. As he looked up, Daniels saw a squirrel frantically leap across the lane. Its front paws grasped the outstretched branches on the other side, before disappearing amongst the leaves. It was so quiet now that sounds like those made by the frightened squirrel seemed magnified, snapping through the static air. The wind had gone now, and the overhanging veil of smoke seemed to hang, as if painted against the sky in faded water-colours.

So intense was the silence filling the lane that Daniels felt as if he could hear something faint in the distance, unreal and yet seemingly real somehow. It was probably his imagination deceiving him, he thought as they strolled down the lane. The trees obscured any sign yet of the village, and it would be at least fifteen minutes, he knew, before the first low, sunken roof would appear through the leaves.

Daniels knitted his brows as he suddenly listened with greater intensity. Surely there was something... something faint back behind them, though Julie did not seem to have heard anything.

"*Ma dheantar aon scriosadh...*" The words seemed to steal insidiously through the air. "*...gearradh lot no milleadh ar an ordu, feadfar diultu d'e a ioc...*" Daniels felt a shiver of recognition, dim and primordial.

"What's the matter?" Julie had taken him by one arm. He felt faint, and there were beads of sweat trickling down his forehead. He closed his eyes for a moment and said that he was all right, though he knew that he wasn't.

"It's nothing," he said. As he spoke, he heard the vague words again.

"*...gearradh lot no milleadh ar an ordu, ar an feadfar, ar an...*"

"Can you hear something?" he asked finally, unable to hold the question back any longer.

Julie laughed, puzzled at his intense seriousness, and shook her head.

"Apart from a bee somewhere nearby, nothing," she told him. "Nothing at all. Why? Should I?"

Daniels clenched his fists as he thought again of the dream that had been haunting him all day. He caught again the far off, half heard singing.

"*...aon scriosadh, creo milleadh, ar an ordu...*"

Was it nearer?

"I can hear something," he said. "I can hear them chanting. I heard them last night when I was here. I can hear them now. I'm sure of it."

"You're imagining things," Julie insisted, dismayed at the way in which her husband's reason seemed to be disintegrating before her eyes. His face was pale and shone with perspiration as he nervously glanced back over his shoulder down the lane. What was he imagining now? she wondered. "There isn't any chanting," she insisted again, with an attempt at firmness. "It's in your mind."

61

He shook his head, unable to ignore the sly whispering through the trees. It was as if they were surrounded by the unseen chanters, hidden behind the undergrowth.

"Look," Julie told him, "if there was anything to hear, surely I'd be hearing it as well."

"Perhaps," Daniels said, doubtfully. Wouldn't the sounds just stop for a moment so that he could think? They seemed to slide intrusively into his mind, *into his thoughts.*

"Won't they stop?" he shouted suddenly.

Julie tried to calm him. She looked into his eyes beseechingly, her face paling with apprehension.

"What's the matter?" she asked as he tensed, listening, though not listening to her. And for the first time, as she watched him, she could hear something too. What was it? she wondered. Someone singing? But no, that was ridiculous - too ridiculous!

Daniels seemed to be straining, as if he was trying to block out the words from his mind. Perspiration trickled down his forehead. His fists were knotted tight.

"...aon scriosadh, minon a d'horga, aon e..."

The sounds were more distinct now, nearer. There was no mistaking them. Julie felt a shiver race down her spine as she looked about herself through the surrounding trees.

"...ma dheantar aon..."

Nearer now, clearer, sibilantly piercing the stillness of the air.

"John," his wife whispered, "what's wrong? What is it?"

Daniels gritted his teeth. He turned around to face Julie.

"I don't know what it is," he said at last with an effort. "I can only tell you what I feel. And what I feel is that there's something wrong, something *horribly* wrong. There's something evil in this place. Laugh at me if you like, but that's what I feel."

"I'm not laughing," Julie replied. "There is something... something strange... something horrible. I can feel it myself now. And those sounds!" She pressed her hands against the sides of her head, as if to seal them out.

"...ar an ordu, ar an..."

"We've almost an hour to go before the bus arrives," Daniels said. "Somehow, I don't think we'll be there to meet it unless we can get some kind of sanctuary in the meantime. Something will happen. I know it will. The villagers - or some of them, at least - were here last night. Why, I don't know. But, in some way, I know we're involved. I'm certain. They did something to me. God knows what it was, but I'm sure it was something. I can feel it inside me." He pounded his forehead with the heel of his fist. "Something deep inside me. Deep. So very deep..."

The chants oscillated, ringing through their ears. As they hurried down the lane, it was as if the chanters followed them through the surrounding forest. Daniels tried to ignore them, but they were too loud now, too insistent. As they came at last to the edge of the village they paused. Daniels pointed to the jutting grey spire of the church.

"We'll go in there till the bus arrives. I'm sure we'll be safer in there."

The tall, dark elms cast a welcoming shadow of tranquillity about the church as they pushed open the iron gate into the grounds and hurried towards it. Daniels breathed in the purer air of the place as the chanting died into an unintelligible, insect-like drone behind them. What doubts he might still have had about the nature of whatever it was that was wrong with the village were dispersed as they experienced the spiritual peace and sense of tranquillity which the bare, stone walls of the church contained within them.

When they finally regained some of their composure, as they stood in the stone-flagged porch, looking out across the churchyard back towards the lane they had hurried along, they saw a man walk out from it, heading for the gate facing them. His heavy greatcoat hung untidily from his rounded shoulders. Even as he watched him, Daniels noticed more of the villagers making their way up the narrow, winding, cobblestone street from the quay towards the church. They seemed to be carrying heavy bundles in their arms, held tight against their chests. When they reached the gate a few moments later, Daniels realised that they were carrying bundles of wood. They tossed them on the ground by the gate, before conferring with the man and glancing now and then at the church, at the same time making peculiar signs across their chests with the tips of their fingers, as if they were somehow warding something off. Daniels frowned; more of the villagers were heading up the street. Like the first ones, these too were carrying bundles of wood.

"What are they doing?" Julie asked, apprehensively gripping tight onto his arm.

He shook his head, unable and unwilling to conjecture, to face all the fears building up inside him.

"I don't know," he said as the second batch of villagers reached the gate, casting their bundles of twigs next to the others. While most of them then returned to the village, others remained about the churchyard wall, like sentinels.

The sky was starting to darken now, as if a storm was on its way. It was appreciably colder, and they shivered as they watched the flaccid and unhealthy faces of the villagers staring at them from above the rough, stone walls about the church. The leaden sky seemed to match the pasty, grey pallor of their flesh.

Daniels glanced at his watch.

"The bus will be due any time now," he said. "Shall we make a break for it?"

There was no choice. If they missed the bus they would be stuck here till tomorrow. His left arm about Julie's shoulders, Daniels pushed the door open and they stepped out. As they did so, the villager stood guard at the gate brought out a pick handle, clenched with both hands.

Julie pressed back, frightened, against her husband's chest.

"We'll never make it," she whispered.

Grunting something, Daniels led them back through the porch into the church.

"It's obvious what those bastards want to do," he grunted, trying to fight back his fears. "We can't stay here indefinitely, yet they won't let us leave."

"What do they want of us? Why are they trying to keep us

here?" Julie asked, close to tears as she peered through the open doorway, back across the path through the churchyard to the gate, where the man stood waiting, staring back at them with a cold, unwavering gaze.

Daniels remembered his dream last night, and he knew that he could not reply. The villagers had always struck him as degenerate, unhealthily so, but there was much more wrong with them than that, something far worse than the excesses of inbreeding. He thought of the cheesy, hair-covered bodies he saw cavorting before the bonfire last night. He realised just how grotesquely similar they were, in a hybridly abortive way, to the demonic goat above the fire, with their excessively hairy legs and satyr-like faces, their yellow eyes burning with unholy and hideous lusts. Although he had never been a deeply religious man, he had no doubts now but that what he saw above the fire was the incarnation of a devil, of the goat-headed spirit of some Hellish and damnable satyr. He shuddered with revulsion. So far the villagers had made no attempt to communicate with them. It was as if they had no real use for speech and were indifferent to it. Had they degenerated so far, he wondered as he watched more of them silently making their way to the churchyard wall, that they were now little better than beasts?

The sky had darkened considerably, almost as if the sun had sunk beneath the hills and the blackness of night was gathering about the sheltered village. There was a feeling of expectancy in the air, an electrical, tingling lull.

In the murky light the villagers seemed to coalesce into a single, indistinguishable mass. As he peered at them he thought he saw the brief flare of a match. A moment later, in confirmation, flames began to flicker in the gloom. The crackling of burning wood broke through the silence, and a cloud of smoke rose into the air. More flames appeared from about the churchyard walls. Daniels realised that they must have set fire to the bundles of twigs. But why? Did they intend to try and smoke them out of the church?

The flames grew brighter. Suddenly the bundles of twigs

were hoisted into the air, and Daniels saw that they were being held aloft on pitchforks by the villagers. A moment later they started to scramble over the walls, pushing through the trees towards the church. Daniels slammed the heavy, oak doors shut, pressing his shoulders against them.

"They're going to try and burn the church down," he cried out. An instant later there was a crash as glass was shattered in one of the tall, stained-glass windows, and one of the bundles flared through it, multicoloured fragments of glass cascading down amidst the flames. Sparks erupted fiercely over the pews underneath like incandescent waves of lava as more bundles were thrust through the windows. Daniels knew that the wood must have been soaked in petrol or some other highly flammable liquid. Thick clouds of smoke billowed out, filling the church with an acrid, unbreathable stench of burning. Daniels saw one of the pews ignite as flames spread like a darkening, blood-red, iridescent stain across it.

"We've got to get out of here," Julie screamed. Wild-eyed, she scanned the smoke-filled, flame-ripped shambles of the church as more bundles of sticks were thrust through the windows.

Daniels took her by one arm and said:

"When I open the door, we'll make a dash for it. Maybe - just maybe - they'll not see us in the smoke. But stick close to me. We mustn't get separated in the confusion." He reached for one of the half-burnt bundles of wood and tore out enough to form a heavy torch. Then, with one last pat of reassurance on his wife's shoulders, he flung the doors open. One of the villagers was stood outside, waiting. A look of devilish satisfaction lit the man's face, his lips curling back from his teeth as his fists tightened about the heavy stick he was holding like a club. The next instant his mouth was contorted with agony as Daniels thrust the smouldering end of his torch into his eyes. There was a hideous scream, and the man reeled uncontrollably backwards, clutching at his face. Daniels kicked him hard in the kidneys as he went down, then turned to pull Julie after him as they ran across the churchyard for the wall. He could hear the chanting again now, but it wasn't clear. Smoke obscured everything, and with this and the glowering darkness of the sky, it was difficult to see. Savage blades of fire were mercilessly cutting through the church roof now as if through an enormous cardboard model, and it would not be long before it was a raging, self-consuming inferno. His only hope was that the bulk of the villagers would think that they were still trapped inside.

There was a rumbling of thunder, which seemed to reverberate through the ground as if from deep beneath the earth. It was difficult for Daniels to believe that it was still midday, so dark was the sky. Any moment he expected a sudden downpour of rain to drench them.

"Which way is it to where the bus comes in?" Julie asked as they scrambled over the churchyard wall, its old stones crumbling beneath their fingers. Skidding on the cobbles underneath, they ran down the street into the village. Daniels looked at his watch. Was there still time to reach it? he wondered frantically.

"That way, I think," he stammered, indicating a narrow street that curved off to their left between rows of tiny, tumble-down cottages, their walls all but hidden by mats of climbers.

Somewhere he heard what sounded like a horse galloping across the cobbles. Thunder rumbled yet again, deep and sonorous, echoing through the wooded slopes of the valley. The hoof-beats came again. Nearer this time.

"Run!" Daniels cried as he tugged at his wife. "Run!"

Something loomed ahead of them through the smoke. It was the back of the single-decker bus, its rear lights piercing the gloom as it started up. Together they made a dash for it, but it was already driving away from them.

"Wait!" Daniels shouted as the gap lengthened between them. Its shadow merged into the smoke as it trundled round a bend in the street. Tree boughs reached out from the hedgerow as the smoke dispersed on the outskirts of the village. "Stop!" Daniels shouted, but he knew that it was too late. They couldn't hear him. The bus was already going out of sight. It gathered speed as the driver changed gears up the hill.

"...ma dheantar aon scriosadh..."

The chanting seemed to surround them suddenly. There was a further clattering of hoofs that echoed deafeningly through the village.

A dim figure shuffled towards them. It was the man who had spoken to them the night before. His insalubrious features shone with sweat like the belly of a long dead fish, white and puffy.

"'E's claimed you," the man said, and he pointed at Daniels. "'Is mark 'as been laid on your flesh an' you are 'Is. Don't fight against 'Im. Don't try to lock 'Im out."

"You're mad," Daniels growled. "You're all mad. Every last one of you. God knows what insane sickness has corrupted this village, but it must've rotted away what little sense you had left. No one, no *thing* has laid its mark on me."

The man laughed quietly, still slowly stumbling towards them, his baggy trousers singed and tattered, his unfastened overcoat hanging from his bony shoulders as if it was several sizes too large.

"'Is mark is there," he replied, unconcerned by Daniels' denial. He placed one of his blackened, diseased-looking fingers at the back of his neck. "'Is mark is there. Where it can grow," he went on ominously. "Where it can grow."

Julie gasped something beside him. What was it she whispered? The lump? *The lump!*

"NNNOOO!" Daniels cried, hurling the torch in desperation at the man, as if to block out his words.

There was a further clattering of hoofs. They were near, now, only just out of sight, he was sure.

Daniels turned around to Julie.

"We'll get out of here even if we have to run all the way to St. Auban."

"You defy 'Im uselessly," the villager called out mockingly as they ran along the lane in the same direction in which the bus had gone only minutes before.

"...gearradh lot no milleadh ar an ordu, ar an feadfar..."

The black storm clouds were boiling up from the horizon in

even thicker, even denser formations, till they smothered the sun. As the light faded, so the chanting seemed to grow still louder, so the hoof-beats seemed to spread still further and further from the church, into the village and countryside.

As they ran, Daniels felt the chants slide into his mind, blocking his thoughts. He shook his head. In front of them he seemed to see something tall and black watching them. When he concentrated on looking at it, though, he saw that it was nothing more than an old, dead tree. *Why did he keep thinking that he must stop and return to the village? Rites? There were no rites for him to perform. The tree. Yes, it was there again. It was only a tree. Why did he imagine that it was something else? Ridiculous! Keep running. Can't let them catch up.*

MUST PERFORM RITES, THOUGH. MUST!

WHAT RITES?

Daniels tried to keep his thoughts straight, but ideas and impressions kept assailing him.

WHAT RITES DID HE KEEP THINKING ABOUT?

His fingers clenched as if to take hold of a knife. Realising what he was doing, he opened them. He felt sweat bead his face. He strained against the alien thoughts and urges that were infiltrating his mind as he stared ahead of them.

There was that figure again. Black goat's legs. Hoof-beats. No, there was nothing there. A shadow. That was all. Just a shadow!

With increasing difficulty, they hurried up the lane. The smoke followed them implacably. The sly, insidious and piercing chants continued to pursue them, as if they were stalking them like some sort of prey. Black goat images continued to flash through his mind. Again and again. He remembered the dream. *No, that was rubbish. RUBBISH!*

It came over him suddenly. For an instant he felt short of breath, and he wondered if he was about to collapse. The hoof-beats returned. They seemed to clatter within his head, hammering his thoughts into oblivion. He caught hold of Julie's arm and swung her round in front of him. The smoke closed in. As Julie screamed uncomprehendingly, he felt something cold being pressed into his hand. With instinctive rapidity he raised it. Something hot and wet gushed across his hand. He heard a scream. It was far, so far away, lost as if through vast and echoing caverns. He saw Julie's face turn grey before him like a papier mache mask. Her mouth opened, slowly, straining the muscles in her cheeks. Something red blossomed out of it, slithering towards him, splashing his face as he moved his hand further. There was a resistance. He looked down and saw the thick red blood that oozed across his hand and about the hilt of the knife that was tightly clenched in it, jammed against the base of his wife's ribcage through her clothes. A goat-like human head, etched with a look of demonic triumph, superimposed itself in front of his eyes, as he forced the knife up till it cracked through her ribcage and she fell against him. The chanting grew into a crescendo of sound.

"...ma dheantar aon scriosadh..."

Blood dripped onto the ground. The sky became black. Boiled. Lightning crashed across the heavens. Ahead of him, over the sinking shoulders of his wife, Daniels saw the satyr watching him, its arms folded across its chest, its goat's mouth gaping as its long, red tongue slid sensuously across its teeth.

He looked round. The villagers, their degenerate features alight with an unhealthy semblance of joy, emerged from the smoke. He knew that he was one of them now.

Now and forever more...

ROMERO'S CHILDREN

Senator Hardy launched an attack tonight against the widespread use of the age-retarding drug OM (Old Methuselah), in which he condemned black market sales. "No one today knows what its long-term results will be. It may halt aging in the short term, but it will be years, perhaps decades before anyone can say that its usage is safe or does not have possible side effects which no one at this time can predict. People take this drug with the hope of a longer, healthier life, but they do not know if this is all they will get."

One of the last newspaper reports ever published in the United States

The old man could hear them scratching and clawing at the outside door two floors below, trying to get in. He'd been able to hear them for the last few nights as he lay in bed, trying to keep warm on the thin mattress of the old cast iron bedstead, with its well-worn blankets and hard pillow. But the door was strong. It would take months for them to wear it down and he felt secure enough to lie listening to them without any fear. Let them waste their energies. He was safe, if neither comfortable nor warm.

The next morning, his joints aching, Jack climbed out of bed and put on his clothes. Although the sun rose several hours ago, it was wintry and pale and gave off little heat, and the cold of the threadbare carpets, scattered like rugs on the bare floorboards, chilled his feet as he trod across them. He rooted out his boots from where he discarded them last night when he drunkenly made his way to bed, and tugged on the socks he'd stuffed inside them, then the boots themselves. He yawned, scratched for a minute or two, then padded across to the window. Its dusty panes looked down onto the street.

They'd gone. Romero's children nearly always disappeared when the sun came up. They preferred the night, with its darkness and shadows. In daylight they were easily seen and picked off. Even their dim minds were aware of this, self-preservation kicking in to make them hide.

Jack put on his padded outer jacket and slipped on his gloves. Snow was on its way, though he didn't need that to appreciate how cold it was. He reached for the rifle propped against the wall, safety catch on, one shell in the breach. Although he felt secure up here at night, there were always accidents – and enough survivors had been complacent in the safety of their homes that they ended up as meat.

Less than twenty years had passed since OM made its first appearance and still they were paying for it. And would till long after he turned into maggot food, Jack thought as he set about unlocking the series of doors that led down the stairwell to the street. He had installed them at the top of each flight, with spy holes through which he could see if any of *them* had gotten inside the building. That had only happened once so far. One night he had been too tired– or drunk, if truth were known – and left the door onto the street ajar. There was a large piece of wood still screwed to the last door at the bottom of the stairs to cover the hole he'd blasted through it – and through the head of the thing mewling on the other side, its beautiful, youthful, dirt-stained face visible through the fish-eye lens.

OM. It was hard to remember it now as anything but a curse that had destroyed everything. Brought an end to all the calamitous fears of Global Warming too, since few cars, factories or anything else mechanical or electrical had functioned for years. Yes, we sure put a stop to that all right, Jack thought to himself ironically. Something to be proud of, at least.

He pushed an eye against the spy hole of the outside door and peered onto the street. It was a rarely needed precaution. And as usual there was nothing there. Just the permanently parked cars, their tyres long since flattened, while rust ate at their bodywork. There were streaks of ice along the road. And the inevitable debris.

With a sigh, Jack unlocked the door and pulled it open. It

72

was heavy, and shut behind him with a resounding thud, before he locked it again. He swung the rifle from his shoulder and took a careful look in every direction.

In the distance three figures were running towards him. The nearest was a girl. He recognised Candice Roe at once, a hard-bitten seventeen-year-old from the settlement. And a damned good shot with a rifle. Which puzzled him. Why was her gun clenched in one hand when she was being pursued? It wouldn't be like Candice to have run out of ammo. Like most people these days she would carry at least a dozen rounds, stuffed in bags or in her pockets – anywhere they would fit. Ammo meant survival. Especially against stinkers.

Jack hurried towards her. He could see she was tiring, and it looked as if the creatures were gaining on her. They were a man and a woman, their unwrinkled faces grey with years of accumulated dirt, dried food and blood like flaking masks of mud.

Dropping to one knee, Jack aimed his rifle at the nearest, centring the cross-wires of the telescopic lens on one eye. He eased back the trigger. The shot took away most of the upper cranium in a spray of brains, bone and discoloured blood. He took out the other a few seconds later. Both lay twitching on the street when Candice reached him, gasping for breath.

"My rifle jammed otherwise I'd have taken them myself," she panted. "Must have run over a mile before I saw you. Gave me a second wind."

"Good job you did. Looked to me as if they were gaining ground."

"Persistent bastards. Comes from not having brains enough to know when you're exhausted."

Jack chuckled. "Stands to sense there must be some compensation for being brain dead psychos. That's just one of 'em."

Candice scowled. "Glad it amused you, Jack."

"It'll amuse you too as soon as you've got your breath back."

"And forgotten how close I came to becoming meat for those bastards."

"And that," Jack added, his humour dying a little. It was a danger all of them had to live with, and one that no one took lightly. They'd all seen the aftermath too often for that.

"How come you're out here by yourself?" Jack asked.

Candice regarded him edgily. "You're a fine one to ask that."

"That's my choice. One I've lived with for years. Wouldn't suit everyone, 'specially these days. But you're not a sad, dried-up old loner like me."

"No." Candice gazed down the empty street, with its stone-clad apartments, shops and offices, all of them derelict. "I just needed some time by myself for a while, that's all."

Deducing it was probably something to do with a boy and none of his business, Jack shrugged. "Okay by me. You can hunker down here for a while if you like. Leastways, I can help fix your rifle. And lend you a handgun. You should always have one as backup. Me, I have a Colt automatic. Stops 'em dead in their tracks every time. I'm not much of a shot with it, mind, but at close range I don't need to be."

"I usually have something. I just wasn't thinking today."

"Not thinking is what gets you killed." Jack gazed down the street, aware suddenly the cold had begun to sink into his bones. "I'm off after some fresh stores. D'you want to lend a hand?"

"Suppose that's the least I could do," she said, an uncertain smile twitching about her lips. "What's it today? Wal-Mart?"

"As always. Canned section."

They walked down the street in silence for a while till they turned onto the car park at the nearest store, with its abandoned cars and the skeletal remains of several hundred bodies, a grim reminder of just how turbulent times had been when the after effects of OM showed themselves.

"How come you never took OM?" Candice asked as they passed the first of the bodies. "There aren't many people your age around these days. Almost everyone of your generation took it. Why didn't you? Religious reasons?"

Jack shook his head. "My wife. We were both in our fifties when OM hit the headlines. She'd already started with

74

Alzheimer's by then. What good is a drug that'll retard ageing to someone with that? Putting off old age indefinitely isn't much of a lure for someone whose brains are turning to mush. Me, I couldn't take it while Rachel was like she was. Didn't seem hardly fair somehow. An extra forty or fifty years of life didn't appeal to me then. Hell, even suicide wasn't far from my mind when Rachel passed on, that's how bad I felt."

"You were lucky."

"You could say that, though I don't reckon as I would necessarily agree. This isn't exactly how I saw my Golden Years." Jack gazed across the car park. "It was bizarre how greedy folks were for it," he said a moment later. "It was never licensed by the government, you know. Most of it was sold on the black market - a black market that became huge quickly, the demand was so big. Things went insane. Everyone wanted it, especially those who'd passed their thirties. Made the profits during Prohibition small potatoes, believe you me. Made some criminal empires enormous. For a while, at least."

"Till its after effects destroyed them too."

"Destroyed everything – almost. There'd been warnings, of course. Some scientists spoke out against OM. But they were ignored. Immortality was too big an incentive for anyone to wait till all the tests had been completed – tests that would take years. Too many years for most folk. Hell, if OM had come along earlier, when Alzheimer's was something that happened to other people, not to us, I expect that me and Rachel would have taken it too. Why not? We'd have leapt at the chance of putting a stop to ageing and gaining all that extra time."

"And you'd have ended as stinkers too."

"Without a doubt. Never heard of anyone who took OM without that kicking in seven, eight years down the line. Made Alzheimer's look like a dose of flu. You think we've got it bad, girl, you should have seen what it was like when there were millions of the bastards going off the rails. Looking back, it's hard to imagine how any of us survived. If'n they hadn't been such dumb bastards I don't suppose we would. Luckily, they were more often as interested in tearing each other to pieces as attacking us. Cut their numbers down a lot in the first year till some of them started working together, those that were left. The *smart* ones."

"I can't remember any of that," Candice said. "I was only a baby then. Lucky for me, Mom was only eighteen when she had me and hadn't thought about taking OM then. Before she could, it all went to Hell."

"How is your mom?"

"Okay. Feeling her age these days."

"If she's feeling her age, imagine what I'm feeling." Jack gave her a sideways grimace, then tucked the rifle under his arm, ready to fire. They were only a few yards from the main entrance to the abandoned store. Its doors had long since been reduced to splinters. The dark interior was a vast array of tumbledown shelves and scattered produce, filled with shadows. "I don't expect to come across any stinkers here. They tend to prefer somewhere less well-trodden to hang out during the day, somewhere less likely to get them shot."

"They know that well enough," Candice said sourly.

"Those that've survived this long know it. There were a lot in the early days too dumb for that. I suppose it was survival of the fittest. The dumbest were culled early on."

"So we've the brightest, eh?" Candice laughed. It was a sound that helped to lighten Jack's spirit somehow. He hated scavenging through derelict stores for the few undamaged cans of food still left in them. It depressed him. Candice's presence helped take away some of his gloominess. Perhaps he'd made too much of his preference for solitude. Now he was getting older perhaps it was time to enjoy some company for a change; maybe even join the settlement. They'd asked him often enough over the years.

You can't do penance for having outlived her forever, he told himself as he looked back on the last few days of Rachel's life. Ironically, her passing had coincided with the first of the stinkers. Romero's children.

If only they'd known how widespread it was going to be, all those politicians and scientists who had appeared on television, discussing the first cases of violence wreaked by the stinkers. The irony was that most of these people became stinkers too in the next few months.

Romero's children had sounded like a joke at first. Except these creatures weren't movie zombies. Not the shambling, ugly, walking corpses the great director had portrayed them as. They were neither shambling nor ugly. Nor dead. Far from it, Jack thought. But they were deadly all right. Just as deadly as anything ever dreamt up in Hollywood.

"Careful," Jack cautioned as they stepped inside the store. He eased some of the tension from his trigger finger as he scanned the poorly lit interior. He had been here often in the past. Knew almost every untidy pile of mouldering food that had been spilled onto the floor from burst bags and ruptured packets. In a few years there'd be nothing left worth scavenging. The alcohol went long ago. Fortunately, he had another source for that. One no one else had stumbled on yet.

Something scuffled deep inside the store, and Jack swore softly as he automatically fell into a crouch, gun at the ready, his eyes scanning the gloom.

"What was it? A rat?" Beside him, Candice held a knife in one hand.

Jack shook his head. "I don't know. There are enough vermin about. But that didn't sound like a rat to me." He passed her his Colt, then crept along the aisle, his head twitching from side to side. If there were stinkers present, he was confident of taking two or three of them easily enough. But there was always the chance a nest of them had decided to camp here. He had on occasion come across a dozen or more – though that was rare. The sensible thing would have been to get help. But that wasn't Jack's way. He'd been a loner too long to break old habits easily. And with Candice as back up, he felt sure they could handle up to four, maybe five between them without breaking into a sweat.

"Over there," Candice whispered. She jerked two fingers

leftwards. "Behind the freezers. I saw something there. It's watching us."

Which was damnably odd behaviour for a stinker, Jack thought.

"You sure it's watching us?"

"Looked like it to me," Candice whispered back. He could tell she was disturbed. She had been brought up dealing with creatures like this and probably knew their behaviour as well as him. "Perhaps it isn't a stinker."

Jack didn't know. Could be someone else scavenging for supplies. But why hide? It would have been obvious who Candice and he were the moment they stepped inside the store. For a start off Stinkers didn't carry guns. Stinkers didn't talk either.

Coming to a decision, Jack stood up and advanced towards where Candice had pointed.

"If'n you're one of us step out," he said. "I'll hold my fire. We only shoot stinkers."

Even though the face had recently been washed, Jack could not mistake what hesitantly stepped out of the shadows in front, its hands above its head in an awkward gesture of surrender. It would take more than a few wipes with a wet rag to remove the years of ingrained grime from the creature's face.

For a moment Jack faltered. He knew he should aim and fire. He could have done that in a split second. Instinct tugged at nerve endings, urging him on. But he didn't. He couldn't.

He waved Candice's weapon down when she stepped up beside him.

"Why?" Her question was half bewilderment, half accusation.

Jack shook his head, uncertain. "Something odd about this thing," was all he could think to say as he stepped towards it, his finger still hooked about the trigger of his gun, aimed at waist level ahead of him.

"Who are you?" he asked.

Her clothes were tatters, held together by grease and dirt,

which clung like a grimy, obscene skin to her scrawny body. The woman took a cautious step from where she had been hiding. Her fingers were black with crusts of blood and grease, the accumulated debris of a thousand meals eaten raw. She was a stinker all right. Jack was certain of that. But her face, especially her eyes, was wrong. There was fear in her eyes. And confusion.

"You hold it right there," he told her. "One more step and, like it or not, I'll fire."

The woman came to an unsteady halt. She was trying to speak. Jack was certain about that. But her tongue and jaw muscles moved awkwardly as if from lack of practice.

"What the fuck is it doing?" Candice asked.

"Damned if I know." Jack squinted through the gloom. Like every stinker he had ever seen she looked youthful. However old she may have been when she first took OM it had stopped the years from gaining on her, even though nearly two decades had passed since she took it. The drug may have messed up her brain, but beneath all the accumulated filth her body was as perfect as the day she took it.

"Awake…" The woman spoke in a stutter, her voice thick, as if her tongue was too large – or unaccustomed to the motions it was being forced to make. "Night…mares…gone…"

"You're the fucking nightmare," Candice grumbled, her eyes venomous as she stared at the woman. "We should cap that thing."

Gently, Jack touched the girl's arm. "Easy now," he said. "Stinkers don't talk."

"Then what is she if she isn't a fucking stinker?"

"That I don't know," he said. "But stinkers don't talk. I know that, if I know nothing else."

The woman swayed. She looked as if she hadn't eaten in days.

"Awake…," she repeated.

*

While Jack heaved a sack of canned goods on his shoulder, most of their labels unreadable, Candice led the woman back to his place. The stinker's hands had been tied together in front of her. Jack had relented on this precaution. If he hadn't, he suspected Candice would have used the slightest excuse – an unsteady step or an odd movement – to open fire and kill the thing.

"You're taking one hell of a risk taking this thing back to your place," Candice grumbled.

"We'll see," Jack said, unsure why he trusted the woman. But somehow, though, he did. Perhaps it was the pain, the confusion and the look of horror in her eyes that convinced him. He didn't know. Less than an hour after discovering her, though, she was sitting in a bath of warm water in Jack's apartment. Apathetically, she let Jack, and then Candice set to work scrubbing decades of grime from her thin body. For the most part the woman was placid, either through exhaustion or fear or both. After a short time, she looked almost human again. Or would have except for the fact she was unnaturally youthful and too mature at the same time despite the tiredness and fear on her face. The woman's hands, especially her fingers, had blackened lines of grease and blood that would take more than soap to remove. Like Lady Macbeth, Jack thought to himself, her sins would haunt her in her hands for years to come.

He gave her a pair of trousers and a jumper to replace the shreds of clothing they had peeled like layers of diseased flesh from her body. The mess had reeked so much Jack had been forced to open one of the windows and toss them out into the street, though the apartment still had the unmistakable stench of Romero's children. They weren't called stinkers for nothing, he thought.

"What next?" Candice asked after the woman had been led into one of the bedrooms to rest.

Jack shrugged. "See if she'll eat some of our food. That's the ultimate test. Stinkers aren't interested in normal food."

"Just off the bone with the pulse still pumping," Candice said, more than a trace of bitterness in her voice.

"Never seen one eat cooked food, even when it was available."

"So, if she does, she's cured? Is that what you think?"

"Maybe."

"Would you trust her then?" Candice glanced at the closed door to the bedroom the woman was in.

"I don't know," he said. "I'd have to hear her talk. Hear her story. See what she's got to say for herself. Weigh it up."

It was dark by the time they were sat about the table. Jack had prepared a thick stew from some tinned potatoes, beans and meat they'd brought back from the store. He placed a bowl of it before the woman, along with a spoon. There was a feeling of tension as she stared at it for several moments, and Jack saw Candice's hand stray towards the Colt still tucked inside the belt of her jeans. Uncertain, the woman grasped the spoon. It shook in her fingers as she awkwardly held it between her fingers, then dipped it in the bowl, before slowly lifting it towards her mouth, spilling half its contents. She stopped as the edge of the spoon touched her lips, as if she was struggling to remember what came next. Then she pushed the spoon into her mouth. Some of the stew spilled down her chin but she barely seemed to notice that. For a moment what was left of the food rested inside her mouth, and it looked to Jack as if she was tasting - or testing - the oddity of it. Or trying to recall when she last had food like this. Cooked food. Seventeen, maybe eighteen years was a long time to remember. Could he remember what the food he ate back then was like?

After gulping what remained on her spoon, the woman surprised him by going on to clear her bowl with an appetite that made Jack wonder how long it was since the last time she ate, though he tried not to think what that meal might have been. That was her past. This was her present. Her different present, he hoped.

When they'd finished eating, Jack eased his chair back from the table and regarded the woman. Her complexion looked better now – more normal, he thought. Almost.

"Do you recall your name?" he said.

Though physically she looked no more than thirty, Jack knew she had to be fifty at least. Nearly twenty lost years of madness lay between the last time she'd used her name and now. It was easy to forget this when looking at her youthfulness.

"They – they called me – Lucy – once."

It was painful to hear that voice. It jarred with her face. A fractured, husky whisper, it made Jack's hair rise on the nape of his neck. He could see the same reaction in Candice. Which was worrying, he thought. Maybe practice would ease a more acceptable sound into the woman's voice.

Jack nodded to Candice. He introduced her to the woman. "My name is Jack."

Lucy repeated their names as if to memorise them.

"How long have you been back with us?" Jack asked. "Since the nightmares ended, I mean."

"Days – nights. I was – frightened. I hid."

"What do you remember?"

She closed her eyes and shuddered. "Nightmares. On and on… endless… nightmares."

"Before then, before the nightmares started?"

For a moment Lucy opened her eyes. She stared at him as if struggling to search back through the decades, then burst into tears. They streamed down her face unchecked. Even Candice looked concerned.

"Easy now," Jack said, quietly. "No need to struggle. If you can't remember, it doesn't matter. If those memories are there they'll come back with time."

"If you want them to," Candice said.

That night, while they lay in separate rooms, Jack heard the scratching outside again. Lucy might have come through whatever Hell she had been to, but others were still living it.

Eventually, though, he slept.

It was three, perhaps four in the morning when he awoke, aware the sounds outside had stopped. Realised they were wasting their time, he thought, though those bastards had time enough to waste, he thought to himself, aware of the irony.

He felt a chill in the air, and he wondered if the window had slipped open. But he was reluctant to leave the warmth of his bed and walk to it, knowing how bitterly cold the air would be. He opened one eye and was surprised to see how light it was. It had snowed overnight, and the building across the street was coated with piles on every ridge and window ledge, reflecting moonlight into his room. It was then he heard something move. Instantly he was wide-awake. He reached for the rifle he had left against his bed. It had gone. Prickles of alarm shivered through his body as his hand reached into emptiness. He moved his head and scanned the room. He saw a figure by the doorway, staring at him. It was Lucy. He recognised her even in the gloom. She was holding something in one hand. It was dark and round. In her other hand he saw the glint of a blade. It was broad like one of the high-tech butchers' knives from his kitchen. His breath caught in his throat as his eyes adjusted to the gloom. Beyond her he could see two other figures in the open doorway. At the same time, he recognised the smell that wafted from them. Had she gone downstairs and opened the bottommost door to let them in? Her fellow "children". Down the front of her clothes Jack saw the vomit that had begun to dry, of the stew she must have thrown up as she lay in bed as the nightmares came and took her again.

Jack swung out of bed, though he had little hope without his rifle. But in the top drawer by the window he kept a handgun. If he reached it, he would have a chance. But the thing, that had briefly been Lucy again, flung the object she held in her hand across the floor at his unshod feet, tripping him. Sprawled helplessly on his back, Jack cried out as he recognised Candice's face staring up at him from between his feet.

Lucy moved towards him, her grease-stained fingers hooked like claws.

SWAN SONG

Bennett shuddered with revulsion.

Sat on the park bench like a pair of old scarecrows rescued from a refuse dump, the couple made his flesh crawl. They were old, filthy, dressed in clothes that were dropping to pieces. Tramps. That was what we used to call them, Bennett thought. In the good old days when you could still call a spade a spade. What did they call them now, with all their PC crap? Bag people? Still too close to the truth probably. Homeless? Bennett hated that word. It sounded like someone should pity them, not despise or hate.

Bennett grimaced. He could smell them from here, still yards away from them. People like that shouldn't be allowed in the park, polluting it with their vile presence. Why didn't the council recruit guards to keep scum like these two out so that proper people, *decent* people, could enjoy it in peace?

Bennett glared. Somewhere inside their rags he knew they would have bottles of alcohol hidden away. A man and what passed, he supposed, for a woman, both of them getting on, like a pair of geriatric mummies, all skin and bone. Neither of them looked as if they had washed in years; ingrained filth dulled their skin.

Bennett thrust his hands deep inside his overcoat pockets as if he wanted to keep as much of his flesh protected from contamination as possible. His fingers itched. In a properly organised society scum like these would be shot. In his imagination he could visualise doing it. Two headshots, that's all it would take, before their carcasses were carted off to some kind of communal grave to be sown with quicklime and covered in dirt.

Bennett had a vivid imagination.

Though divorced, childless, a self-confessed misogynist, he never felt lonely. A group of cronies at the pub in which he spent most of his nights looked on at him in admiration. They admired the erudite tone of his wit with an awe that tickled his vanity. Once, years ago, he had been a schoolteacher. He had been forced, though, to take early retirement. He had been a good teacher too, even if he did ruffle a few feathers. Not like these namby-pambies nowadays who let their pupils do whatever they liked, leaving school with no more idea of good grammar than some Johnny-come-lately from Wogga-Woggaland. Bennett had known how to keep discipline. There had been no slouchers in his classes. No fidgetters. No cheek.

Bennett's eyes bored into the couple. He expected they would stay transfixed to that bench till they'd guzzled whatever they'd brought with them, then sneak away to buy some more – or steal it.

With an effort of will, Bennett walked past.

With any luck they would be gone tomorrow, and he could enjoy his stroll through the park in peace.

The next day, though, they were there again. This time they had brought a flask and a plastic box of sandwiches, lying between them on the bench as if they were having a God damned picnic. Now and then one of them threw a handful of crumbs across the tarmacadammed path for the birds. A flock of pigeons were already pecking at them.

Bennett grimaced. Pigeons were another of his pet hates. They were no better than rats. Feathered vermin. Typical that the old couple should be feeding them.

"Excuse me," Bennett said. He stopped in front of them, regimentally ramrod. The steel ferrule of his rolled umbrella tapped the ground for emphasis. "There's a by-law against doing that." He flicked his hand at the crumbs scattered across the path. "No feeding. You could be fined," he said.

For a moment there was a look of incomprehension in the old couples' faces as they stared up at him. The man's mouth, purple with some kind of growth, like a rope of vein running under his lips, part hidden in stubble, moved into a smile. Bennett felt unsure about it. Was it threatening, half-witted, or an attempt to placate him?

Unused to uncertainty, Bennett nodded his head in an affirmative gesture. "They take it seriously," he said. "There are notices all around the park." Somehow, he realised, he sounded defensive, as if he needed to justify his admonition, even though neither of the old couple had said anything yet. Just that stupid smile from the man, that meant what? Anything? Nothing? Bennett would have preferred a straight forward argument. That he could cope with. That he would have relished. That he knew he would have won. What he could not deal with was this incomprehensible smile. He felt intimidated by it, though he failed to understand why.

"Just be warned," Bennett said after a moment's silence, abhorring himself for it, knowing that he would run over what he had said – or failed to say – the rest of the day, dissatisfied with it. It was something he was not used to experiencing. Inadequacy was anathema. It showed weakness, lack of moral backbone, and cowardice. Things he despised.

He was still seething when he reached the Red Pheasant, a public house across from the main gates into the park. Although he didn't normally drink so early in the day, he felt the need for one now. A stiff brandy to steady his nerves. That was the ticket. Something to take his mind of those scumbags.

"Make it a large one, landlord." He rested his arms on the well-polished bar.

"You look as if you need it." The landlord's world-weary sack of a face had seen too many late nights and not enough sleep.

Bennett growled. "It angers me when people abuse our parks."

"Vandals? I hadn't heard of any trouble."

Bennett shook his head. "A couple of old tramps. Sat like the King and Queen of Sheba. You'd think they owned the place." Bennett frowned; he could feel the landlord's eyes stare at him as he handed him his brandy.

"Wouldn't be a man and a woman?"

Bennett bridled at the man's hushed tone.

"As it happens, yes. Customers of yours?"

The man shook his head, laughing. "You wouldn't find them here, oh no. Not that I'd want them."

"Of course not," Bennett said, wondering. He could sniff the landlord had more to say. Bennett had a nose for nuances, developed over years of dealing with two-faced, duplicitous children. "What do you know about them?"

The landlord leaned over the bar with a conspiratorial air, even though the only other customers were sitting around a table at the far end of the room, too far away to hear. "They're not what you think." The man tapped the side of his nose. "Some say they're worth a friggin' fortune. I wouldn't know about that. But they're well off, that's for sure. How rich?" He shrugged in a gesture that reminded Bennett of a Jewish comedian. "They live in one of those Edwardian villas down Maple Road. It used to belong to the old man's father. In a bit of a state now, I believe."

Bennett frowned. "They're rich?" Somehow this made him dislike the couple even more. They had less reason to be as they were. What kind of degenerates were they? Drop-outs? Hippies?

"I'll have another brandy, landlord." Bennett passed him his glass. He felt he might need lubrication to get the brain cells working on what he'd heard. "Have one yourself," Bennett said. There was a smile on his lips that was foxy and cruel. Might as well see what the landlord had to say about that pair. The more he knew about them the better.

An hour later, Bennett left the pub. He knew he had drunk too many brandies and would suffer later. But it had been worth it.

"They used to be great philanthropists, you know," the landlord had said. "Caused a bit of a kafuffle, though, which brought it to an end. That was when they ran a refuge of sorts in town for homeless people."

"Appropriate enough," Bennett said. "They dress like a pair of vagabonds."

The landlord laughed, perhaps dutifully. "That was before I took over this pub. I didn't live round here then so I only know all this from hearsay. It was around the time I moved here that there was a bit of a scandal." He leaned closer, his breath a tad too close to Bennett's face, but for once he ignored this. "They used to take some of these homeless back to their house, give them a bed to sleep in, fed and clothed them, then sent them on their way with enough money to start a new life. That's what they claimed. Word was, though, that some of these buggers were never heard of again." The landlord shrugged. "You could say why should they? Most of them probably slipped to their old ways again. End of story. Trouble was one of their progenies was different. He wasn't a dropout who'd made a mess of his life or been kicked out by his parents. He came from a good family, had gone to university and almost completed his degree when he had a nervous breakdown. Went right off the rails. Abandoned university and disappeared. His parents were frantic to find him. Thought something bad must have happened to him. The police had photos of him on TV. There were articles in the papers. His parents even hired private detectives to track him down. He was finally traced here. He wrote home to his parents. Just a postcard, if I remember right, to say he'd met some people who were helping him." The landlord winked. "You can guess who."

Bennett nodded his head as expected, wondering when the blasted man would cut to the chase.

"Anyway, the lad's parents contacted the couple and asked about their son. Left weeks ago, they were told. Have no idea where he is now. That's what they said. Trouble was, no one had heard or seen him since that postcard. Well, that was it. A proper shit storm erupted, if you'll pardon the French. The police got a search warrant and for days the house was screened off as they went through it like a dose. Dug up the garden. Made a right proper mess of it, they did. I heard tell every floorboard inside was lifted. Even walls were knocked through in case there were hidden chambers."

"And?" Bennett asked when the landlord paused to replenish their drinks.

"Not a sausage. No trace anywhere. No trace of anything

suspicious at all. Red faces all round." The landlord smirked. "Not that this did the couple much good. Gossip was they might have buried the lad's body on the moors somewhere. Too much about their odd lifestyle came out in the press. No one had known till then they'd been into the occult. That all came out, with photos of statues and stuff in their house they'd bought from all over the place. Leaks about some of the books they had on Black Magic and stuff like that didn't help, of course. There were all sorts of rumours suddenly, most of them probably a load of old bollocks, but shit sticks, doesn't it?"

Purposefully Bennett strode towards the park. By the time he reached the bench they'd occupied earlier the couple had gone. Back to their villa, no doubt, resenting the idea that they could live in the kind of grandeur he'd had described while all he could afford, after a bad divorce and a reduced pension from the Education Authority, was a maisonette. Life was so bloody unjust. If there was a God, He was a fickle, hard-hearted bastard, unfair and perverse. Otherwise degenerate scum like the Huntingtons would never be allowed to live in a house like that. Work all your life, scrimp and save, slave to pound what knowledge you could into ungrateful minds week after miserable week, and what was your reward? The answer gnawed at Bennett's bowels like an incurable cancer; he felt tears of frustration in the corners of his eyes.

It just wasn't fair.

It wasn't fair at all.

*

Bennett spent a sleepless night, vexed by thoughts of the couple, as a result of which he was late getting up in the morning. His head ached from the brandies he'd drunk in the Red Pheasant – and from more he'd drunk back home, staring at the bars of his electric fire. The crisp air helped to clear his head when he ventured out. If nothing else he had his health. He could still do a brisk walk around the better parts of town.

Whether it helped his peace of mind to gaze at houses he could no longer afford, he was not sure, though it did him good to feel as if he belonged amongst them, not the one-bedroom rabbit hutch he rented. His divorce had left a few thousand in the bank, but nowhere near enough to buy a house of his own. What money he had would see him out if he took care. Though, damn it, he knew this just wasn't really good enough. He had worked all his life and should have been able to spend his remaining years with enough money to splash out on luxuries if he wanted to. The only pleasure left was the occasional Martell he would buy at the supermarket along with his groceries. And the four or five nights he spent each week at the pub.

Although Bennett knew he should have avoided going there, he could not help it. Walking past the end of the park, he carried on towards Maple Road, with its large, stone-built Edwardian villas, erected during an era of ostentation. Bennett loved buildings from that period. He could have lived during those golden years before the First World War with equanimity. It was his ideal time - before socialism spoilt it all.

His heart grew heavy as anger rose in his throat. Bennett stopped in disbelief at the large, sandstone gabled house, knowing it had to be the one that belonged to the couple. From the weathered varnish on its otherwise splendid door and window frames to the dilapidated shrubs that filled the surrounding garden, it stood out from its neighbours. Sun bleached curtains were drawn at most of the windows and it looked abandoned, an eyesore compared to the rest of the houses here.

The filthy scum! How could they?

Bennett felt the injustice more keenly still.

As he stood at the rusting cast-iron gate, he could hear music. Old pop music, sixties stuff, just what he would have expected. A Wagnerian, Bennett still recognised it. *Nights in White Satin*. Overrated, degenerate trash, just perfect for a pair of ancient hippies, high on drugs.

Now that he had seen the house Bennett returned home, his

feelings in turmoil. They were still in that state when he went to the pub that night. The Foxhill was quiet but at least "Pinky" Pinkerton and Sam Nedwell were already there. Bennett took his whisky and water to their table.

A retired accountant, Pinky was treasurer for his local Conservative Party Association and a staunch admirer of Bennett's wit. His sallow face and downturned mouth would twist like rubber whenever he chuckled at one of Bennett's blistering comments. The stem of a pipe stuck out of the top pocket of his sports jacket. A self-made businessman, who Bennett knew had never been quite as successful as he tried to make out, Sam Nedwell was red faced and portly. Sporting a pale cream Armani suit too many years out of date, it was already starting to look a tad grubby at the cuffs. Bennett had known both men since their schooldays.

"What's troubling you?" Sam asked in his blunt no nonsense way.

Bennett downed half his whisky and pulled his face. He told them about the tramps in the park.

"Down-and-outers, eh?" Pinky said with a knowing nod.

"Bloody no good fucking drop outs," Sam retorted.

The three men shook their heads.

"But rich." Bennett looked at his friends in turn. "Filthy rich."

"Bastards."

"All inherited," Bennett said, dismissively. "Never earned a penny of it themselves. Had it left to them by the old man's father, who's probably turning in his grave right now."

"Spinning, more like" Sam said. "It's stuff like this makes me glad I've no sprogs to squander what's left of my money when I pop my clogs," though Bennett and Pinky knew to the contrary. Sam had sown more than his fair share of wild oats in the distant past. In his younger days he had been a bit of a lady's man, not that anyone looking at the broken veins littering the cratered knob of his drinker's nose would think that now.

"If they keep feeding those pigeons, you should report them," Pinky said.

Sam shook his head. "They'd get nothing worse than a warning. What good's that?"

"Not good enough, that's what. I want to do more than that," Bennett said. "They're a disease."

"You know what you have to do about them." Sam's watery pale blue eyes stared into his. "Diseases, I mean, old man." he added the grunt of a laugh more pig-like than human.

Pinky frowned. "Inoculate against them?"

Even Bennett laughed this time, having caught Sam's gist. "Eradicate them."

"Like that advert on TV," Sam said. "You know the one? It's got those blasted germs all wallowing around in the toilet bowl. In goes the bloody cleaning stuff, whatever it is, and they burst apart, bloody well killed, the lot of 'em." He leaned back, laughing.

"My wife wouldn't watch any channel but the BBC," Pinky said. "I still don't. Haven't seen an advert in years."

"You don't know what you're missing." Sam wiped tears from his eyes. "Better than the programs half the time."

"Perhaps that's why Pinky's wife would only watch the beeb," Bennett said.

Pinky laughed, his jaundiced face contorting with delight. "Got you there, Sam. Scotched you, you old reprobate."

Sam snorted. "You're probably right. Might be why I spend more time here." He raised his beer in mock salute.

"What do we do about the tramps?" Pinky said, cocking an eye at Bennett.

"What do you mean *do*?" Sam's face became serious again. "It's years since we did anything like that, if that's what you mean."

"Ten years at least," Bennett said. He didn't need to say more. Starting in their mid-twenties, Bennett and Pinky fresh from university, Sam on his way to his first fortune, ducking and diving, they had been drawn into radical politics "so far to the right even Attila the Hun was out of sight" Bennett used to phrase it. The spark was when Sam had broken a picket line and an angry mob of strikers had beaten him. He was making a huge profit supplying a firm with raw materials to help blacklegs keep production going. Lorry drivers had refused to pass the pickets, but Sam owned his own vehicle and had been offered umpteen times the going rate for what he was taking in. The three friends had always been close at school, ganging up on anyone who tried to pick on them. Bennett, rubbed raw at being forced to join a teacher's union, had been the most vociferous in Sam's defence. Pinky had already gone through half a dozen right wing parties by this time, most of which would have got him barred from membership of the Conservatives for life. It had not taken much to persuade the three to retaliate against the men who attacked Sam, finding out where they lived and paying each of them a late-night visit. Balaclava clad and armed with baseball bats they had broken several arms and legs and cracked a few heads before lying low. They had been careful to make sure they left no clues as to whom they were and no one, even to this day, had ever pointed a finger at any of them.

Encouraged by their success, they had carried out other "commando raids" over the years, targeting anyone who made life hard for any of them. It had worked well. Difficult colleagues at school had been reduced to physical and psychological wrecks, sometimes quitting the profession. Sam's business rivals had found life less than rosy if they infringed too much, while Pinky enjoyed it for what it was, an opportunity to wreak violence, safe in the knowledge they were all too clever to get caught - and too respectable to be suspected. Pinky had an edginess that would have shocked his clients, none of whom would have ever imagined that their sallow-faced accountant had such a streak of sadism in him: it was sometimes so severe, in fact, the others had to rein him in, even though they were almost as bad themselves. If they hadn't, though, they would have had more than four deaths on their hands by now.

"You're not going soft on us, Pinky?" Sam said, breaking the silence.

Pinky had large fists, which he rested on the table. They

would have made him a formidable boxer if he had gone in the ring, but that was not what interested him. Broken knuckles bore testament to the faces he had enjoyed reducing to bloody ruins, far beyond what any pugilist would have been allowed to go even in his day.

"The spirit's willing," Pinky said with a sigh of regret. "I'm not so sure about the flesh."

"Don't I know it?" Sam grimaced. "The quack's told me to watch my blood pressure. It's sky high. Says I should take it easy; cut back on alcohol, would you believe!" He emptied his glass with a flourish of contempt at the thought.

"We're none of us getting any younger," Bennett said. "The days of taking on all and sundry at the dead of night have long since passed."

"I'll drink to that. Or will when I get a refill." Sam glanced at Pinky, whose round it was.

Bennett drew them in over the table. "Perhaps we should end with a swan song." He smiled at his friends.

"The tramps?" Sam grinned with appreciation. "Degenerate old bastards, ripe for the picking. They'd deserve what they get."

"Why not?" Pinky said. He grinned too, and Bennett wondered if his friend was thinking how far they would let him go this time.

This *last* time.

Satisfied at the outcome, Bennett said, "I'll reconnoitre the place. See what's what."

"Why bother?" Sam asked. "If they're like you've described, let's just go in and deal with them."

Pinky nodded his agreement.

Bennett sighed, though he was pleased at their enthusiasm.

*

It was dark when they set out. Fog blurred the light from the street lamps, suiting their purpose. Bennett preferred to be seen by as few people as possible. Midweek, there were not many late-night revellers as they walked past the edge of the park, its gates locked hours ago. They hurried by. Bennett could feel the frost in the air seep through his coat. Not much further now, though. Already he could see the turning to Maple Road.

A car drove past, gone within seconds. Bennett knew its occupants would hardly have noticed them; even if they did, they wouldn't remember.

Soon he was standing outside number twelve, its shambolic garden unmistakeable in the gloom. There were lights behind the downstairs curtains and, standing at the gate once more, Bennett could again hear music inside. More sixties trash, as distinctive as joss sticks or the sickly stink of marihuana. He told Pinky and Sam to wait till he had gained access.

As his friends stepped back into the darkness of the privets, holding their balaclavas, Bennett gripped the top of the garden gate and swung it open. Striding to the door he grabbed hold of the brass knocker and pounded it hard. Echoes bounced back at him.

Moments later the music dimmed inside, and he heard a muffled conversation. A light came on behind the door, before its locks were turned. The door opened and a thin, querulous-looking face peered out; hair hung in a halo on either side of it.

"We spoke yesterday." Bennett's voice sounded oily even to him. "I thought I'd call to apologise." He put on his best smile. "I think I spoke harsher than I should."

The man smiled at him as he let the door swing open.

"Alicia, we have a visitor."

Bennett was shocked at the old man's voice. It was a dismal whisper that made him shiver with revulsion. Worse, the smell inside the vestibule was a rank mixture of vegetable decay, dead rodent and dust. There was a disturbing sweetness mingled with it, reminding Bennett of dry rot. This was so intense that he began to worry how safe the building was. Again he noticed the purplish red vein below the old man's mouth, though it seemed lower this time. The skin around it looked raw as if it had been bleeding. Bennett curled his lip in disgust.

"Come in, come in." The old man wafted Bennett to enter. He wore a threadbare cardigan that hung full of holes from his scrawny shoulders. As his hand urged Bennett in, it was as if his cardigan was woven out of spiders' webs and was ready to fall to pieces.

Bennett slid past, trying to avoid any physical contact. The man revolted him even more inside the thick atmosphere of the house, and for a moment Bennett wondered whether he had made a mistake in coming here, for all he despised the repulsive couple and hated what they had done to this house.

Beyond the vestibule there was little light inside the hallway. Dust and cobwebs snuffed out most of what was radiated by the solitary bulb still working in the chandelier hung from the ceiling. Bennett had more of an impression of what the place looked like than a clear, distinctive view. Shadows clung to its corners, filling them like piles of dust. The carpet was unidentifiable, probably more grime than fibres. He could feel his nostrils cloying with dust.

The old lady appeared from an open doorway. Music resonated from the room behind her. There was a smell of incense. Though normally Bennett despised such stuff he welcomed it now; it overpowered other odours, smells that were almost bad enough to make him nauseous. Perhaps that was why they burned joss sticks, dozens of which were scattered on shelves around the room. Books, mainly leather-bound editions, crinkly with age, shared space with them.

"You were at the park," the old lady said. Her voice had the same breathless whisper - which didn't surprise Bennett. What else could you expect in the kind of stale, dusty atmosphere of the house? It was a wonder they didn't asphyxiate. God alone knew what viruses were rampant here.

"He's come to apologise for what he said to us," the old man said. His hand, no more substantial than a bundle of dead leaves, pressed light against Bennett's shoulder, urging him into the room.

The old lady wore a floor length dress in a style Bennett

recognised from the late sixties or early seventies. A hippy dress. Its colours had been dulled by time and dirt into monochrome. The old lady's arms were wrinkled sticks of bare flesh. Lead-coloured bangles hung from her wrists.

Both were bare-footed, Bennett realised. Purple blotches, like diseased flesh, were the only colour. Their toe nails were thick, like poorly-preserved ivory, yellowed with age.

He swallowed back the bile that burned in his throat as he turned to face the old man, ready to tug the door open so his friends could enter.

Something, though, restrained him.

It wasn't compassion. Or fear of the consequences. By the time anyone found the old couple their bodies would have decomposed so much no trace of the men's presence would remain. Besides, they had no intention of leaving any evidence here.

"Would you care for a drink?" the old lady said.

Bennett stared at her. Now was the time to strike. He felt a burning outrage against them both, undiminished by meeting and talking to them. They epitomised everything that he hated.

Coming to a decision, Bennett turned to face the door when something heavy struck his head.

*

Hours later he awoke to the worst headache he had had in years. Worse than any hangover he had ever had too; he felt sick, uncomfortable, unable to move, and with a pulsing light inside his head that came with regular waves of pain.

Bennett's memories of what happened were vague. He could recall walking to the old couple's house. He could even remember stepping inside, and the smells and dust. The smells were still there, clogging his nostrils like rotting dough. Disgusted, Bennett opened his eyes; they were gritty with mucus and for a moment he could barely see anything other than the vague impression some distance away of a curtained window.

98

Grunting, Bennett struggled to sit up, even though the pain inside his head worsened. He realised that his hands had been tied together. The coarse rope had already worn layers of skin from his wrists and hurt.

His ankles had been tied as well.

Sitting on a kind of low couch like a chaise longue, its upholstered seat was hard to his buttocks and uncomfortable. Finally, after a few minutes, Bennett managed to swivel round till his feet touched the carpet. By now he could make out more of his surroundings. The light came from a naked bulb hung from a plaster rose in the ceiling. Though large, the room was empty apart from the couch. A dim expanse of dull carpet lay between him and the window and he could hear an occasional scuffle inside the walls, either rats or mice. Other than this, the only sound was music, that infernal bloody sixties trash he had heard before, dimmed by distance.

As his mind grew clearer Bennett wondered if the couple had realised something was going on, though he could not imagine what could have warned them. What had happened to his friends? Even if he hadn't opened the door to them, they wouldn't have waited long before bursting in.

As if in answer he heard someone scream. It was a man, crying out in pain. The scream was stifled almost at once as if gagged.

Bennett raised his hands to his mouth and gnawed at the rope. He still had all his own teeth and they were strong and sharp; it did not take long before the rope's fibres parted beneath them, even though he hated the taste of oil and dust in which they had been smothered. It made him feel nauseous.

There was a series of loud bumps and someone laughed. It was neither Pinky nor Sam; perhaps the old man, he thought. Bennett tore away another mouthful of fibres from his bonds, spitting them out. He'd soon have the bastard laughing a different tune when he was free. His teeth dug into the rope once more, tearing at it in anger now.

Spurred on by more bumps, Bennett soon managed to

weaken the rope till he could tear it apart. Throwing it onto the floor, he bent to unfasten the rope around his ankles. Seconds later he threw that away as well.

Taking a few deep breaths to calm his nerves, Bennett massaged his wrists to restore their circulation, then heaved himself off the couch, searching for anything he could use as a weapon. He pulled back the curtains from the window. Its old square panes were coated in layers of grime, though he could still see through them onto the back garden - an untidy jungle of overgrown evergreen bushes, most of them rhododendron black as grottoes. It stretched out for what had to be a hundred feet, possibly more.

Realising he was on the first floor, Bennett wondered how the old man and his wife had managed to haul him all the way upstairs; they had to be a lot stronger than either of them looked to move his weight. Frowning, Bennett returned to the couch. He tipped it over onto its side and started to work on one of its heavily carved wooden legs, forcing it back and forth to wrench it free. It was curved, narrowing to an ornate foot. The wood was heavy and hard. Finally, he hefted the leg in one hand and took a couple of swings. It was no baseball bat, but he knew it would be effective enough.

Breathing heavily, Bennett approached the door. It was locked, as he'd expected. Belts and braces, Bennett thought. He tightened his grip on the couch leg. Much good their precautions would do once he was face to face with them and it would take more than a locked bedroom door to keep him here.

There were more bumps, louder this time. Putting his ear to the door Bennett could tell they came from further down the passage outside. With a grunt, he stepped back from the door, pounding into it as hard as he could with his shoulder. His breath exploded from his lungs and he winced in pain. The door was stronger than it looked. Like the old couple, he thought. Stepping back, he kicked as hard as he could with the sole of his shoe. The door shuddered and he heard something give. A splinter sprang from the doorframe next to its lock. He kicked it again, feeling the tendons inside his calf stretch painfully. He was getting too old for tricks like this, too old and too stiff. But this time, though, he could tell he had almost succeeded. He grabbed hold of the door handle and gave it a tug. There was a mournful creak and the door burst open. Bennett stepped outside in time to catch sight of the old man who had started down the passage from a door several yards away. Bennett ran towards him, brandishing the makeshift club. With a yelp, the old man ducked into the nearest room, but was too slow shutting the door against him. Bennett shouldered it open, gratified to hear the man fall across the floor behind it.

Sam lay inside the room on a bed, gagged and bound. The old lady was knelt over him. Something long and red, like an intravenous drip, hung from just below her mouth. It dangled on Sam's neck, and Bennett was disgusted to see what looked like a mouth at the very end of it open and shut as if it was trying to suck itself to his friend's skin.

Grunting with the exertion, Bennett swung the couch leg across the back of the old lady's head, felling her. He strode into the room, turned, saw the old man trying to scramble to his feet, nursing what looked like a broken arm; Bennett gave him no chance. Once, twice he swung the weapon, crushing his skull with resounding thuds. He felt something give at the second blow. A third followed, but by now the old man was on the floor, his legs twitching as if he was having a fit. Which, Bennett thought, debating whether to hit him again, he probably was. The bloody red vein beneath his mouth had been dislodged and lay on his collar. Something dark oozed from it.

Bennett turned to the man's wife. The single blow to her head seemed to have killed her. This didn't surprise him. It had been a hard one, delivered with all his weight behind it.

Throwing his weapon to one side, Bennett untied Sam's hands. Released, Sam tugged out the lump of cloth that had been bunged into his mouth.

"They've got Pinky in another room," he said, looking sick. "They started on him first. Did you hear the poor bastard?"

101

Bennett had had no idea which of them screamed. The sounds had been too wretched to tell.

Saying nothing, Bennett helped Sam up, then hurried into the room from which the old man had fled. Pinky was lying there, fastened like Sam on a bed. As soon as they saw their friend's face, though, they knew they were too late. Just as they could tell that Pinky had died in terror; it was transfixed on what was left of his features. Part of his face, though, had gone, as if a powerful acid had eaten it away to leave a gaping blood-soaked hole.

"The fucking bastards killed him," Sam muttered, though that was what they had come here to do to the couple.

Still struggling to understand how the couple had managed to overwhelm them, Bennett grunted. It just didn't seem possible. Just as it didn't seem possible that the old man had been responsible for the damage to Pinky's face.

"Did you see the thing hanging from the old woman when she was leaning over you? What the hell was it?"

Sam shuddered, gritting his teeth. "It was obscene." He looked as if he was going to be sick. "It couldn't have been real."

Bennett wasn't so sure. It had looked real to him, *too bloody real*.

They searched the room. There was little furniture inside it, a set of drawers and a cheap plywood wardrobe dating from sometime in the 1950s. They contained nothing more than a few sheets. No sign of any acid or anything else corrosive - or anything that might have been used to carve Pinky's face.

"What happened to the bits that are missing?" Bennett said.

Reluctantly, Sam looked again at their friend's body. Most of Pinky's nose and the whole of one side of his face had gone, as if scooped away.

"It must be somewhere," Bennett said.

But where? And why had the man done it?

"You don't think he ate it?"

"Ate it?" Bennett seriously wondered if his friend had been unhinged by what had happened.

Sam frowned. "Makes you wonder if they might have killed that lad the landlord told you about."

"If they did, why did they? And what did they do with the body?"

Sam shrugged. "Questions no one will answer now."

"I suppose not. We better get out of here."

"And Pinky?"

"Leave him here. It'll be ages before anyone investigates this place."

Already Bennett was working out what he and Sam would do once they left. They would return to his house, have a drink or two to relax their nerves, then make sure they had the same story. The less said the better.

Bennett grunted to himself. At least there'd be no more tramps sitting in the park. Having little empathy, even for his friends, he was not bothered by what had happened to Pinky. He was just one less person he could share his time with at the pub. Beyond that he knew he would barely miss him.

"What was that noise?"

There was a quaver in Sam's voice. Nerves, Bennett thought. He was always the weakest, always the one most ready to cut and run.

Annoyed, Bennett stopped and listened though.

Despite his scepticism, he could hear something too. Not loud, more a rustling, like stiff rushes.

They returned to the room in which Sam had been held. The old man's legs were still twitching. There were other movements too further up his body, beneath the cardigan on his chest. For the first time Bennett began to feel afraid. He could tell that these movements were wrong. There was no sense to them.

"What the hell is it?" Sam said, echoing his fears.

It was as if something – perhaps a lot of *somethings*, all small and spindly – were moving under the old man's clothes. Bennett snatched up the couch leg from where he had discarded it. He edged nearer the old man even though he wanted nothing more than to turn around and run.

"Don't." Sam whispered. "Leave it be."

But he couldn't. He couldn't just leave it. He had to see. With a certainty of movement that belied his fear, Bennett pressed the couch leg against the bottom of the old man's cardigan, using it to push the garment further up his chest. The wool caught on a splinter, making the task easier, till Bennett saw what he was exposing. Neither hard and straight like an insect's legs nor bonelessly muscular as in an octopus, the thick red tendrils writhed in the open air. They were long – longer than he had expected, with mouth-like suckers at their ends. One unexpectedly whipped out at him with uncanny accuracy and he flinched away from it, dropping the couch leg.

"Get out of here." Sam tugged his arm. As they turned, one of the tendrils sprang and coiled like a rusty bedspring around Sam's wrist, clenching tight. He cried out in pain and grabbed at it with his free hand, trying to take hold of it and tear it free, but his fingers could not get a grip on it.

"Help me," Sam cried. His face filled with terror. A second tendril whipped out at him.

Bennett recoiled. Already he could see them climbing free of the old man's chest like a nest of spiders, all legs and no body. A deep cavity lay where they had been. He could see the old man's ribs inside it.

"Help me," Sam pleaded. He tugged at the tendrils, but more of them were fastening themselves to him all the time. They were ridiculously long, as thick as a man's middle fingers, and tough, covered in a kind of carapace. Bennett looked for something other than the couch leg with which to defend himself, but there was nothing.

"I'll get something downstairs," Bennett said, "a knife."

Ignoring Sam's pleas Bennett fled from the room; the air quivered behind him. Tendrils snatched only inches from the back of his neck, trying to grasp him. Sam shouted, begging for him to stop but Bennett slammed the door shut. He ran to the stairs, stumbling down umpteen steps at a time till he reached the hallway. He did not stop till he had left the house and run on, staggering, past the park. Almost blind to everything around him he continued to the town centre, bumping past what few pedestrians there were and almost getting himself run over as he recklessly crossed road after road till he reached his home. Slamming and locking the door behind him, he leaned against it, gasping for breath. His chest hurt and he knew he had pushed himself to the brink of a heart attack. All but falling into his living room he poured himself a large brandy and gulped it down. It burned his throat but helped. He drank a second, more slowly this time as he sank onto the sofa, his hands still shaking. He could not to believe what had happened. It was like a nightmare. He shut his eyes, unable to remove the sight of those hideous tendrils. He could see them lashing themselves round Sam's arms.

It was nearly an hour later as Bennett poured himself a fifth brandy when someone knocked on the door.

Spilling most of the alcohol on his lap, Bennett leapt to his feet.

"Bennett, you bastard, open this fucking door!"

It was Sam, his voice furious.

"You double crossing cowardly bastard. Open this door or I'll kick it in."

Bennett scowled. No one had spoken to him like this for years.

Slamming his glass on the table Bennett strode to the door. What relief he felt at his friend having escaped was tempered by the man's anger. What right had he to accuse Bennett of anything?

Bennett swung the door open. Sam stood, dishevelled, his coat stained with blood.

"God, man, you look like you murdered someone. Get off the street, for heaven's sake. You'll get us arrested."

"Good of you to think of that." Sam's voice was sour. He pushed his way in and glanced at Bennett's brandy by the sofa. "See you wasted no time."

"Have one yourself. You look like you need it." Feeling his anger fade, Bennett followed him in.

105

Slumping onto an armchair, Sam reached for the brandy and poured it into an empty glass. His hands shook so much most of it slopped onto the carpet. Sam looked down at it and smiled. "Sorry about that, old man. It's been a trying night."

Bennett sat on the sofa.

"How did you escape?"

"Escape?" Sam grimaced as if the brandy tasted bad and put it down.

Bennett tensed, feeling uneasy as he studied his friend. Sam's coat was still dripping. The front of it was soaked with blood.

Sam glanced across at him and reached for the buttons down his coat. His fingers were red.

"It won't make much difference," Sam said as if this explained everything. "We can still continue just like before, only better, stronger."

Bennett's face drained of colour. He darted a look at the door into the kitchen. He had knives in there, carving knives. If he reached them, he could kill Sam with ease.

His friend grinned at him.

He pulled his coat open, popping buttons. Coiled like a bundle of dark red brambles, nesting tight against his chest, the creature stirred.

"Those old hippies were hard for them to work with," Sam said. "They had to be pushed and threatened, forced to kill. It went against their principles, you see, the soft old bastards. Damn near starved these creatures to death."

Bennett rose to his feet.

"It'll be easier with us. We don't mind killing, do we? We love it, in fact." Sam grinned. "There are benefits," he added. "Those hippy bastards were over a hundred years old, you know. You wouldn't have guessed it, would you? They were, though. It's quid pro quo, don't you see? There's a payoff. Benefits. Benefits in kind, I suppose. Things work both ways. No more aches and pains. No more muscles creaking with old age. No more bones turning fragile as the years pass by. We'd feel young again, Bennett. *Young and strong.*"

Bennett looked at his friend's chest. The blood was already beginning to clot. There was barely any sign of what hid inside other than a vein pulsing across his chin.

Bennett stared at the creature on Sam's blood-soaked lap. It was already starting to straighten its legs.

Sam's grin broadened.

THE FARMHOUSE

As he left his carriage at the small, country station of Arrendale, to step down onto the platform, Melbury looked around for the nearest porter. Knowing that this was as far as the trains went in the direction he was going, he had intended catching a local bus the rest of the way, but when he asked, they seemed of little use to him unless he was willing to wait until six o'clock in the evening, which he wasn't.

Consulting his map, he asked if it wasn't possible to cut across the hills. "It nearly halves the distance," he added.

The porter, a red-faced man with a cheerful frown, said that he wouldn't advise it. "Bad 'ills to cross, you see. They're nice enough now, but come three and they'll be black with clouds, likely as not. Unpredictable. You wouldn't want to try crossing them. Bleak things to be on in a storm, I can tell you."

Melbury thought a moment, biting his lips till they were white. After eight years of lecturing at college, he was more used to giving than receiving advice. Somewhat tartly he said that he didn't see how the weather would change today. "It looks fine enough to me. Not a cloud in sight."

No doubt noticing the well used rucksack by Melbury's feet and the look of someone who felt himself to be an expert camper, the porter just said: "Maybe, maybe," and left it undecidedly at that.

Leaving the station, Melbury hitched his rucksack well up on his shoulders, put on a pair of Polaroid sunglasses and made his way through the village and out along a lane towards the hills. As he went he could not help picturing in his mind, as thoughts of everyday life were left further and further behind him, how like it was now this landscape must have been in the days of the Celts and Roman legions marching against rebellious Brigantes, of days before cars were invented and horses were the only means of travel besides one's legs.

Laughing to himself at the porter's advice, he strolled along a footpath across the first and smallest of the undulating hills, setting off from its windswept summit to where the sun, now and then, glittered on a meandering stream amidst a gathering of trees.

Feeling refreshed and invigorated by the walk so far after the warm drowsiness of the train, he half ran, half stumbled downhill, ending in a cautious clambering through the tangled undergrowth to thrust his hands gratefully into the cold water of the stream, splashing it across his face. Guelder rose and hazel grew luxuriantly about him with the buttressing trunks of several elms that had long since fallen at sharp angles against their still upright neighbours, brightly putrescent with honey agaric fungi and abundant patches of *Pleurotus sapidus*, alarmingly attractive with their lily-like caps set off against spreading rugs of moss. There weren't many trees, and most further in were lying grotesquely yet pathetically on their sides with their shrunken roots poking the air. Some were completely overgrown with moss, speckled yellow where Jew's-ear fungus had grown.

"Are you lost?"

Surprised, he turned around to see a girl - perhaps eighteen or nineteen - standing some five yards upstream. Like Melbury, she was dressed for hiking, with a heavy floral blouse and blue jeans, a small white handkerchief which she'd just been wetting in the stream, as well as a small, slate-grey rucksack held with one strap on her shoulders.

Taken aback - though pleased by the beauty of her hair, which lay attractively on her shoulders, and by the even contours of her face - he said that he wasn't. "Not really." Reconsidering the lameness of his reply, he added that he was just admiring the view before continuing on his way. "I've more than a good idea of the geography of this place from my map." To underline the point, he took it out of his anorak, making his way towards her, safely if not elegantly across the ferns and slippery stones along the bank. Pointing at the map, he said:

"This is where we are now. I'm headed due east for Kendal. That's just across these hills here. It's not really far as the crow flies. Just a stiff walk."

"And worth it for the view," she said, looking around at the wind-brushed trees.

"Exactly how I feel. I can't stand the lanes. So many cars on them that you might as well be in a city at times. Which way are you going?"

"Fenley. But I've got to go through Kendal to get there."

"Then we can go on together," he said. "It'll make a pleasant walk even pleasanter."

Having agreed, they cooled themselves off at the stream, before wading across it to make their way leisurely uphill. As they talked, he learned that her name was Janet and she came from Cheltenham, using what free time she had before starting work in the autumn to see as much of the better parts of the English countryside as she could. Originally, she'd been with a friend, but they'd had an argument and parted.

Very soon they were immersed amongst the hills. Yet, despite the many features about them, he found her company so utterly fascinating that it was not until they were rising from a valley several hours later when they came upon a farmhouse, that his attention wavered, though even then it was she as much as Melbury who aided this diversion with her enthusiasm for looking at it.

Giving her a hand as they clambered over the debris surrounding it, he joked about the farm's weirdisms: the peculiar angle at which it sloped, the whole building being several degrees off the vertical, the ugly gash in its roof and the fungi that covered its walls like dilapidated veins. Over a colourless door at the front was an embossed stone with the legend 1743 upon it, though it had been worn by age and caustic elements into nothing more than a weather-pitted plaque. Age showed from its every blurred contour as Melbury took out a torch from his rucksack and shone it through one of the grimy windows. "It's so wrecked it must be deserted," he said finally. Inside

111

haphazard lengths of rotting wood were entangled with flaking strips of plaster and even more ragged, veil-like drapes of webs, whilst the gash in the roof was mirrored by an even larger gash in the first story floor, the whole being dulled by damp and nightmarish shadows which resisted the torch beam with a dogged belligerence, loping about the quaking walls as he shone it about the room. In one corner stood the remains of a table, whilst a gigantic hearth leered at them from one wall; a grotesquely shaped thing that was made of iron and served as a fireplace and oven. A repugnant smell of decay surrounded the edifice like a vile miasma, whilst the ground near to it was slimy as though thick with mud.

"I wonder if this is the place all that fuss was about in the papers a few years ago," Janet said after a while, pushing open one of the fragmentary windows as she spoke.

"What fuss was that?"

"Don't you remember? About an artist - what was his name? - Preskett, I think - he painted surrealistic Biblical pictures: *The Four Horsemen of the Apocalypse, Wormwood, Babylon the Great, The Locusts* and things like these. He was supposed to have committed suicide in an old farmhouse around here."

"Supposed?"

"That was what all the stink was about. See that hole in the roof? That was what made me think about it. According to the papers he killed himself by covering his clothes with petrol and setting himself alight, burning half the house down with him. But there was talk of other things besides suicide. Ritualistic murder for one. All very dark and mysterious. I'm surprised you don't remember it. One of the Sundays even did a serial about his life and works, all the juicier bits about his stays in mental homes, divorces, mysticism, drugs, midnight orgies on the hills, of course."

Melbury stood back, looking the old building over. "I think I remember something about it. Slightly mad, wasn't he? This was his retreat."

"But not his last. Somehow even this held something that

made him retreat even further, into death."

Laughing, Melbury said that she made it all sound very mysterious.

"But I mean to," Janet said, laughing too. "Come on, let's have a look inside."

Saying that he couldn't stop her, he led the way carefully towards the door. "I'll go first," he said. "It's not very safe and we don't want an accident in an isolated place like this."

The door gave way quite easily beneath his touch, swinging open wide on its crumbling hinges. The nauseous stench he'd noticed earlier swept up into his face like the belch of something long dead and rotten. It dazed his senses and almost made him lose his balance as he staggered through the pulpy debris that covered the floor inside: the decaying leaves and slime, puffed and discoloured by fungi and mould. Carefully, he ran the torch beam across it, reciting:

> "I spied John Mouldy in his cellar,
> Deep down twenty steps of stone;
> In the dark he sat asmiling,
> Smiling there alone."

"What's that?"

"A poem," he said, with a delicious facetiousness.

"I know it's a poem. Who wrote it? Not you?"

"No, not me. De la Mare. Come on, we'll go on a bit further."

An insipid glow seeped through a gash in the ceiling, making everything grey other than the mysteriously black shadows. At one end of the room began a rotting staircase, whilst near to them stood several small but heavy cupboards, all of which seemed to have been modelled from clay and chunks of dead flesh which had since been left to fester into gangrenous mounds. Partly sickened, partly consumed by morbid curiosity, Melbury looked around at the funnels and cones and hammocks of webs and the pus that dripped steadily from the moss-like remains of the ceiling. In one corner amidst a pile of plaster that had given way from the wall, he noticed a rectangle of red and black. He pushed his way through the rubble towards it.

As he leant over it, he discovered that it was a metal box, much like the ones used for keeping petty cash in at offices.

"Wonder why that was missed when Preskett killed himself?" Janet said as she knelt beside him.

He shrugged. "*If* this was Preskett's home. Besides, I'd say it was hidden in the wall by the look of it." Pushing more of the plaster from the wall, he put his hand into the gap behind. "Quite large," he said. "The rain and decay probably succeeded in doing what a search party couldn't."

Using a stone, he snapped the padlock holding the box lid down and forced it open. Inside were several small books, blackened by damp and stains from the in-running rust. Carefully Melbury picked up the topmost book. Tucked inside the front cover was a sheet of paper. On it, written as though in some haste, was a quotation. Slowly, he read it out loud:

"Out - out are the lights - out all!
And, over each quivering form,
The curtain, a funeral pall,
Comes down with the rush of a storm,
And the angels, all pallid and wan,
Uprising, unveiling, affirm
That the play is the tragedy 'Man'
And its hero the conqueror Worm."

Janet shuddered. As she did so a light film of rain fell through the hole above their heads. Looking out through one of the deep-set windows across the hills, Melbury saw the grey veil of a summer shower covering everything in a myopic blur.

Quickly, they left the farm, deciding as they looked across the darkening hills to pitch one of their tents to give them some shelter till the rain had died down. Deciding on his because it was larger, they erected it and retreated inside as sheet lightning flashed across the hills. Lying back on the ground sheet, Melbury said: "I wonder what all that writing was about?"

Janet pulled her face in false mockery. "The papers did say that Preskett was mad."

"If," he added, "the farm and the writing were his. One

shouldn't jump to conclusions."

"And one shouldn't preach."

After talking for an hour, they lapsed into silence. Rather than brightening, the weather outside seemed instead to be getting even worse, darkening all the time. Already exhausted after the unusual exercise of his trek across the hills, Melbury began to doze amidst half thoughts of inns and warm beds, hot meals and beer. It was with a feeling of profound and lasting shock that a short time later he jolted awake, a strange sense of solitude, of loneliness numbing him as though a deep iciness permeated the air. Towns, railways, roads and people seemed so far away, lost through vague vistas of eternity.

Sitting up, and striving to subdue these feelings, he looked across to where Janet had been lying, but she'd gone. Opening the tent flaps, he leant out into the drizzle.

Melbury was surprised to see how long he'd been asleep.

"Janet," he called, stepping outside. He zipped up his anorak as the wind thrust itself against him. "*Janet!*" When he looked across the hillside all he could see was grass and swaying trees, alive with motion as they were battered by the winds. Still receiving no reply to his calls, Melbury wondered where she'd gone. Prone as he was to worrying, conjectures of the vaguest and, thus, most intrusive type stormed his mind with land sliding rapidity.

"Janet, where are you?"

The only cover in sight was the farmhouse. Besides this there was nothing that could hide her from view. But why should she be in there? Despite all the tales about it, there was nothing of interest in the place.

Pushing his doubts to one side, he called out again. But still there was no reply.

Remembering the deceptive solidity of the farm's buttressed walls, with their gaping cracks, and the burnt beams underneath the roof, the warped floor above, the rotting stairs, all with vivid images of incipient collapse, he felt a growing sense of alarm. Suppressing this with the knowledge that panic would only make things worse, he returned quickly to the tent for his torch. Without it a search would be practically hopeless.

As he flashed it on, he noticed a scrap of paper left where Janet had been lying. Picking it up, he read:

In case you wake up before I get back (or, to be gloomy, in case I have an accident), I'm going to the farm for those books we found. It's stopped raining now, but I don't want to risk them getting absolutely ruined if it starts up again.

Janet.

The paper fell, forgotten, from his grasp as he rushed outside, the air greeting him with an invigorating rush of freshness. Without wasting a second, he ran towards the farmhouse. The books he'd left scattered in the debris fluttered wildly in the winds. A loose leaf from one of them blew against his leg. Picking it up, he saw an etching of great if diabolical quality. It was of a squat, pig-like creature with great knobbly joints, a formidable monstrosity admittedly, yet almost paradoxically showing in such vivid detail pain, agony and anguish on its twisted, entortured face that Melbury winced at regarding it. What Hell must have been the inspiration of this artist? What forbidden delusions, dreams, nightmares had formed within him the inspiration for the ultimate blasphemy peeling, thrusting its nauseous self from the creature's floundering body: the snakelike creatures, the worms that gnawed at it like a cancer, springing from its hoofs, its legs, from its chest and ruptured stomach? Grünewald at his most insane could never have perpetrated such a blasphemy as this time worn etching. The realism was veritably obscene, a mockery of life itself. The very suggestion of what was depicted revolted Melbury, sickened him as confronting insanity would, as viewing the foulest of all the foul deeds carried out by man. It was almost indescribable in its cacodaemoniacal entirety, only the etching itself could reveal what it so successfully did.

He threw away the paper. This was ridiculous. He'd never

find Janet like this. "Janet! Where are you? *Where are you?*" He cupped his hands about his mouth and called again. As his cries echoed claustrophobically through the house, he saw something move in one of the corners amidst a Stygian void of shadows.

"Janet?"

Awkwardly, the girl stepped through the debris into the moonlight fanning through the roof. Her face was pale and still, her arms listless by her sides. It was like the calm tranquillity just after a storm or as one was about to erupt, the peaceful way she stood, statuesquely still in the moonlight.

Relieved, he ran towards her, the torch beam sending shadows fingering about her face, filling her eyes like the profoundest black gems, whilst making her blouse rumple in strangely sensuous ways, with liquescent depths of blackness.

Before he reached her he stopped. Her body seemed to move and yet did not move. Muscles shivered, yet her limbs remained still.

Suddenly he began to scream. He couldn't stop. The whole world dissolved into an oblivion of tearing hysteria.

Something fell from her face. It was long and thin. Her mouth dropped, and yet another slim, slithering object fell from her. Yet another from her hair, though it looked, even in the gloom, as though it came from her eye. One, two, then four as she collapsed upon the floor, hundreds more spreading out from her shrinking body into every conceivable direction, wriggling soundlessly into the shadows.

> *"Out - out are the lights - out all!*
> *And, over each quivering form,*
> *The curtain, a funeral pall,*
> *Comes down with the rush of a storm,*
> *And the angels all pallid and wan,*
> *Uprising, unveiling, affirm*
> *That the play is the tragedy 'Man',*
> *And its hero the Conqueror Worm."*

THE LAST COACH TRIP

Hamer Street Working Men's Club had been in decline for more years than Harold cared to remember. Built around the time of Victoria's death, it had managed to thrive through two world wars, the Depression, strikes, the three-day week, the advent of cinema, radio, even TV, right up until the 1980s. After that a kind of acceleration seemed to set in with cheap beer from supermarkets and the attraction of videos, then DVDs, and its days became numbered. The cigarette ban was the final blow, Harold was sure. Now in his seventies he was sad to think that in a few weeks a way of life he had grown to love would end when the club closed its doors for good.

"At least it'll go with a bang." Eddie nudged him as if he'd read his thoughts. Not that this would have been difficult. The club's closure had dominated their talk for months.

Harold sighed. Tipping the last of his beer into his mouth, he struggled to his feet; sciatica niggled the base of his spine. "Another?" he asked unnecessarily before trudging to the bar.

The main part of the club was a large rectangular room, a cluster of tables and chairs close to the bar, a padded couch down the longest wall by a snooker table, with one armed bandits near the door. These gave the club what profit it made, since its members had long ago made it clear they weren't in favour of paying more than they had to do for their beer, already the cheapest in Edgebottom. Not that this had done much to sustain membership. Perhaps nicotine-coloured walls and foul-smelling toilets had much to do with it, plus no TV, vetoed by the committee whenever the subject was raised.

Harold enjoyed its exclusivity. Its members were mostly working-class men, retired these days, who came here to drink, exchange some gossip and air what wisdom they had about world events with lifelong friends, and perhaps play dominoes, sometimes for money.

"Quiet tonight," Eddie said when he returned with their pints.

"A lot of them'll be saving for the trip." As would he, Harold thought, if he hadn't a bit put to one side in the bank. His pension wouldn't have paid for his nightly visits to the club *and* the trip, not nowadays.

"The last coach trip," Eddie said with disbelieving reverence. "Who'd have thought it?"

"Aye." Harold shook his head, then tasted his beer. Satisfied, he gulped a quarter down, then relaxed, feeling sad. "We should make the most of it," he said. "In a few weeks all we'll have left will be memories."

"I've too many o' them already." Though a couple of years younger than Harold, Eddie had always looked older, his face furrowed with wrinkles down both cheeks. "Still," he said, with a smile that nudged these into curves around dentures too perfect to be real, "the trip'll be a stylish way to end it."

The club's coach trip to Ripon Races had been an annual event for as long as Harold could remember. It was an all male affair that started in the morning with pints at the club till the coach turned up, breakfast at a country pub, then an afternoon of gambling on the nags before a slap-up meal en route to a Yorkshire nightclub and their eventual return to Edgebottom in the wee hours of the morning. Last year, Harold had won over fifty pounds from the bookies, though most of it went on drink that night – and one of the worst hangovers he'd had for years. Still, it had been worth it. It always was.

"There aren't as many of us this year," Eddie said. "There was talk of getting a minibus instead of a coach. They'd have done it too, but there are too many of us."

"It wouldn't be the same in one of those bloody things. We need a full-size coach with plenty o' legroom."

"Like I said, we're going out in style."

Harold grunted. "You make it sound as if we're snuffing it."

Eddie shook his head. "Feels like it sometimes," he said. "The end of an era."

Harold glanced at his friend. He was even more sombre than usual tonight. "You could do with something to cheer you up." Harold reached in his pocket, counting his change. "Here – I'll get us a round of Glenfiddich. That'll do the trick."

*

It didn't seem long before the weeks passed and Harold was sitting at his usual spot a yard from the bar, waiting for the coach to arrive. He'd arrived early wearing his Sunday best. Feeling lucky today, he'd drawn a few extra pounds from the bank and was going to have the kind of afternoon with the bookies he'd only ever dreamed about in previous years, going out in style, as Eddie said. He worried about Eddie. He had become more morose over the last few weeks. He'd lost weight too, though he'd never had much meat on his bones. The club's pending closure had seemed to depress him even more than the rest of the regulars. Not that any of them were jumping around with joy. Harold was too old to start going into pubs again. Apart from their trip to the races, he had only ever drunk in the club for years. And from what he'd heard he'd missed nothing. Revamped, their insides gutted, most pubs had been turned into drinking holes for snotty-nosed youngsters out to get pissed or been turned into licensed restaurants. The old-fashioned backstreet pub was a thing of the past. Like workingmen's clubs, he thought. Harold shook his head. He would probably end up drinking cans of beer in front of the telly, something he had never done before in his life except at Christmas. Alice would turn in her grave at the thought.

Harold glanced at his watch. It was time Eddie was here. Growing concerned, Harold glanced around the club. Despite the smoking ban there was a haze around the bar. Big Bill Entwistle and his chums were leant against it, puffing away at cigars. No doubt they were going to finish in style too, Harold thought as he glanced around the faces of those who were here. Only Eddie was missing. Which was worrying. Eddie was never

121

late for anything. Ever.

Grimacing at the ache in his back, Harold pushed himself to his feet. He gulped down the last of his beer before wandering to the door. As always it felt strange to be looking out onto the cobblestone street at this time of day. A few more minutes and the coach would be here. Harold stepped outside and looked up the street towards Eddie's house, but the only figure was a paperboy burdened with an oversized bag. Come on, Harold thought, agitated now. They had talked so much about today he couldn't believe that Eddie was late. They had left the club early last night so they would both be fresh this morning.

"Where's Eddie got to?" It was Frank White, another veteran of more than forty-year's membership. He rubbed the bristly nostrils of his nose and peered outside, squinting as if sunlight hurt his eyes. Broken veins trailed across cheeks the colour of weathered putty.

Harold shrugged, unwilling to think what might have delayed his friend, but knowing it had to be serious.

"You don't think he's ill?" Frank stared at him with too much concern for Harold's taste. He didn't want to think down those lines yet.

"There's time. Coach isn't due till eight-thirty."

"He's cutting it fine. Driver won't want to hang around. He's a schedule to keep."

"He'll hang around if he has to," Harold said. "Eddie's paid his dues like everyone else."

"Everyone else is here."

Harold shook his head. "He's not late yet."

"Too late for a pint afore we set off." Frank beamed with triumph. "First time he's missed in thirty year."

Harold was tempted to go to the bar and order Eddie a pint to wipe the smirk off Frank's face, but it would be petty – and pointless. If Eddie wasn't here by now, he more than likely wouldn't be here at all. Deep down Harold knew this. He wondered if he should go to Eddie's house to find out what was wrong. Stubbornly, Eddie still hadn't had his phone reconnected two years after it was cut off. "If I can't pay for it now how the 'ell do you think I'll manage in future?" he said when Harold tackled him about it. Harold told him he was being pig-headed, that you never knew when you might need a phone in an emergency. Harold hoped there hadn't been one today, though he knew nothing less could have kept his friend from being here.

There was a rumble as the coach arrived outside. Hydraulic brakes hissed as it stopped beside the club.

Too late, Harold thought as the coach's shadow loomed inside the club through its dappled windows. He glanced at his watch, then hurried outside. "Driver, wait a few minutes, will you? I'm going to see what's held up my friend. He should have been here by now."

"I am," a voice behind him said.

Shocked, Harold spun round, twisting his hip. He felt a chill down his spine.

"You daft bugger. D'you want to give me a heart attack?"

Eddie grinned. "I got here as quick as I could. I overlaid."

And looked it. Chalky stubble showed that he hadn't even shaved. Or put on a tie, Harold realised, though Eddie was never seen without one. "If you were thirty years younger I'd be asking where you'd spent the night."

"Thirty?" Frank said, waddling over. "More like fifty. What you been up to, Eddie? Birding it?"

Eying the liverish look on his friend's face, Harold said, "Leave him alone. He's here, isn't he?"

"So long as he isn't sick when we set off."

Frank walked away, laughing.

"Take no notice of the sarcastic bastard," Harold said.

"Never have." Eddie leaned against the outside wall.

"Are you all right?" Harold asked. "You don't look so clever."

"Felt better." Eddie took a deep breath. It wheezed down his throat, disturbingly deep.

"Do you want to give the trip a miss? See the doctor? I'll go with you."

123

Eddie laughed. "I wouldn't ask that of you, Harold. I don't want to miss it either. There won't be no more, you know."

Harold helped him up the steps into the coach while the club steward and several committeemen loaded boxes of sandwiches and crates of beer into the boot.

"I think we'd better sit near the front," Harold said.

"In case I'm sick?"

"You never know. I might need to get off quick myself. Those beers I've had are weighing heavy. They might've been off."

A few minutes later the rest of the party climbed on board. Fewer than on previous trips, there were plenty of seats for everyone.

"Next stop The Farmer's Glory," the driver called as he set off. "Full English - for those who can manage it."

Eddie dozed most of the way to the pub. Harold kept an eye on him, not happy with his friend's jaundiced face. At The Farmer's Glory, though, Eddie recovered, grinning cheerfully. "I feel hungry enough to eat a horse."

"You'll have to make do with bacon and eggs."

"Hope there's a damn sight more than that on our plates," Bill Entwistle said. He squeezed down the aisle, eager to be off. "We've been promised Full English."

Despite what he'd said, Eddie barely seemed to touch his food.

"You'd think it was the condemned man's last meal," Frank joked. He dabbed his lips with a napkin. "It's the last breakfast we'll have on trips like this," he said, his eyes mournful. "Might as well make the most of it."

Which sobered the mood.

"Cheer up," Harold said, taking a folded copy of *The Sporting Life* out of his pocket. "Let's pick some winners."

In an attempt to lift everyone's mood, Harold managed to persuade them to have another round at The Farmer's Glory before they trundled back to the coach. The weather was fine, with a brisk wind to freshen them up when they went outside, but Eddie soon began to feel dozy, the soft motions of the coach lulling him to sleep.

He woke up as they pulled into the car park of The Feathers. It was half an hour from the racecourse, but they always stopped here for lunch.

Eddie gazed around, barely interested in his beer. Taking it all in for the last time, Harold thought. It would hit him hard when it was over, when all they had left were memories, especially when the club closed too. Harold dreaded that. It was hard to accept change at their age, especially when it was something that had been a big part of their lives for decades.

"Have you picked any winners?" Harold asked, but Eddie shook his head. "That's not like you," Harold said. "You've usually filled your card by now. You're slipping." But Harold's attempts at humour seemed to have no impact. Please yourself, Harold thought, determined that his friend's mood swings weren't going to spoil his day. He had worried about Eddie catching the coach and had looked after him as attentively as he could since then, concerned about his state of health, but it was his day too. If Eddie was determined to stay in this obtuse state of mind, so be it. There was an afternoon's gambling and drinking ahead and Harold wasn't going to miss any of it for anything.

Which he didn't, even though most of his horses failed to fulfil his hopes. At least there was the beer, and the weather stayed fine. He saw Eddie now and then, but his friend seemed to be in a world of his own, wandering aimlessly. Harold never caught sight of him with a drink or near the bookies, which seemed bizarre. What was the point of coming to the races if you weren't going to have a few bets or a pint of beer in the fresh air?

By the end of the afternoon Harold was thoroughly exhausted, teetering on the right side of drunk. Better still, his last race had come up trumps and a twenty-pound bet had returned him a hundred. More than recouping what he'd lost, it cheered him up tremendously. Though he rarely if ever made a loss at the races, breaking even was almost as good a way to finish as any. So, he felt as he ordered a pint at the bar and looked around the crowds to see if anyone from their coach was there. He needed someone with whom to brag about his win.

Which was when he saw Eddie.

Like a lost soul drifting amongst the crowds.

"Eddie!"

Harold hurried after him before he was swallowed up again and took hold of Eddie's elbow.

"What have you been up to all afternoon? Have you won any bets?"

There was a worryingly detached look on his friend's face – so detached it seemed to have smoothed its wrinkles and made him look, if anything, younger, in mind at least. Which worried Harold even more. The word Alzheimer's sprang unbidden – and he wished it hadn't. Could the club's closure in a few weeks' time have brought it on? Harold didn't know enough about Alzheimer's to be sure, but he feared the worst as he stared into Eddie's eyes. There was a fey look in them. "He's been talking to the faeries," his mother would have said. It made Harold feel uneasy. Was he going to lose his closest friend as well as the club?

"Are you all right, Eddie?" he asked.

"Never felt better." Eddie smiled. It was calm and placid, a man at peace with the world. Harold doubted if Eddie had ever borne a smile like it before in his life. Scorn and cynicism, sourness and disdain, these were Eddie's usual moods, not some loopy-doopy hippy bliss as if he'd swallowed a happy pill and won first prize in the National Lottery. Harold knew then that his friend must have suffered a breakdown. That was what they called them, wasn't it? Breakdowns? He was sure it had to be the club's closure that had caused it too. A widower like Harold, it was all Eddie had left in his life. Which was a bitter thing for Harold to think about. Was he any different except that he hadn't cracked up yet? Though he knew there were other ways events like this could affect men their age. Decline, loneliness, and death, these were more likely, he knew. A fine old way to end your life, he thought as he drew Eddie towards the bar. Perhaps his friend was the lucky one.

"Here, sit down and I'll fetch us a couple o' pints." Harold guided Eddie to a vacant seat in the open air not far from the bar. Like the rest, the table beside them was awash with an afternoon's spilled beer. Cigarette ash flowed through it like industrial waste.

Quieter now that most of the course's punters were beginning to head for the car park, it wasn't long before Harold returned with their drinks. He placed Eddie's down in front of him.

Eddie gazed at it, smiling benignly.

"Thanks, Harold." He didn't pick it up though.

"Bloody Hell, what's happened? Have you signed the pledge? It's for supping, not admiring. It won't get no better the longer you leave it."

As if to set an example, Harold knocked back half his pint in one swallow, though he knew he should be taking it easy now till they'd had the dinner they'd booked en route to Dewsbury. There were hours of drinking ahead of them when they got to the nightclub. If he wasn't careful he'd end up legless. It was years since he last slipped up and drank too much, though he still had a scar next to his eyes where his glasses had cut his face when he fell in the toilets of the club they'd gone to, too drunk to stand. He was taken to the local A&E to get stitched and been left to spend the rest of the night by himself in the coach till they set off home hours later. That had been a trip to remember.

Harold put down his glass. He decided to leave the rest, even if his friend did make him want to get blathered. Why did this have to happen today? Why couldn't Eddie have stayed all right till tomorrow? It wouldn't have mattered then. He knew it was selfish to wish this, but it just wasn't fair. It was his last day at the races too.

"Come on, Eddie," he said, feeling guilty. "If you don't want your beer we might as well go back to the coach."

"What's up with him?" Frank asked when they'd returned to their seats. "Too much to drink?"

Harold bit back his annoyance. "He's not been feeling good

all day." He glanced at Eddie's vacant gaze as he stared through the window at the passing crowds. "I don't think he's even had anything to drink."

"So you say," Frank said with a chuckle. "Looks like he's had a skinful to me."

Which was something even Harold began to suspect when they arrived at the restaurant for their evening meal. Eddie barely touched his food, even though Harold suspected he'd had nothing to eat all afternoon. He'd even refused a teacake when they stopped at The Feathers before the racecourse.

Perhaps because of all the alcohol he'd drunk, it didn't seem long to Harold before the meal was over and they were off again for the Revellers Night Club. It wasn't Harold's cup of tea, but it was part of their tradition. There was a stand-up comedian and a baby-faced crooner they were told got through to the semi-finals in last year's *The X-Factor*, though Harold didn't remember him. Not that he was bothered. The last few hours of their last coach trip were drawing to a close and, despite the drinks he'd had all day, he felt melancholic. He sat down at the table they had commandeered as far from the stage as they could get, where they could ignore the acts if they wanted to and talk instead, reminiscing over the day's events.

"Off his ale," Bill said to Harold, sotto voce. He nodded at Eddie. "Not his usual self. Last year we had to carry him to the coach." Harold remembered that night. None of them had known there'd only be one more. They'd enjoyed themselves in style that night. Really enjoyed themselves, Harold thought. Tonight was turning into a wake.

"Come on, Eddie. Liven up," Bill said.

Eddie looked at him and smiled. He'd smiled a lot today, Harold thought. Probably more than he'd done for the past decade. Which wasn't natural. Not for Eddie. Nor him either. Not that he'd had much to smile about except when his horse shot past the finishing line a length ahead of its nearest rival.

"Perhaps we should organise a trip of our own," Frank said. But they knew it wouldn't be the same. They'd talked about it time and again over the past few weeks, but they'd drift apart when the club shut down. It was their focal point. There was nothing to replace it.

"This is our last trip," Eddie said. He said it simply, so matter-of-factly it silenced them all for a full minute. The men exchanged glances, then slumped in their seats as the stand-up came on.

Harold felt unnaturally sober when they finally headed back to the coach at two in the morning. There was none of the usual raucous jokes or attempts at singing. He'd seen livelier funerals.

"The end of an era," Harold heard someone mutter though he couldn't tell who. It sounded resentful. Had the day been so bad? Harold rubbed his eyes, feeling old and tired. His shoulders were heavy. They weighed him down. He reached for the handrail and hoisted himself into the coach; the coldness of the air inside chilled him. It was worse than out, as if the driver had left the engine running with the air conditioning on full blast while they were in the club.

Eddie pulled himself up the steps behind him.

Fog had drawn in by the time the coach left to weave its way through the dark streets, heading for the road that would take them back to Lancashire. Dry stonewalls blurred by as they ascended Saddleworth Moor, sometimes hidden by rolls of mist that drifted towards them. Vehicle headlights were diffused through the fog, blinding one second, then gone the next. Harold didn't envy the driver his job. It had been a long day for him too and conditions were treacherous. Which was probably why he sat upright at the steering wheel, stiff with tension.

Harold glanced at Eddie, who was smiling to himself, contentedly.

Eddie turned and looked at him. "It's been a great day, hasn't it? A day to remember." Unexpectedly, Eddie pulled himself to his feet. He swayed unsteadily. His hands gripped the back of the seat behind the driver as the coach swung round a bend in the road.

"Driver!" Eddie's voice was discordant, loud. It drowned the hubbub of conversations in the coach behind him.

What the hell was he up to? Harold slid across the seat to stop him.

"Don't distract the driver," Harold said in a harsh whisper, but he was already too late. Startled by the tone of Eddie's voice, the driver turned. At the same time headlights flooded the windscreen.

"No!" Harold heard himself cry as if from a distance, dismay and fear paralysing him as a lorry's horn, loud as a ship's, blasted through the air.

"No what?"

Harold looked up from his beer. His eyes felt gritty when he opened them. Eddie was standing beside him, looking down.

"Are you all right?"

Harold felt befuddled. He was sitting in the club, its door wide open only a few feet away. A coach stood outside. Its windows glinted in beams of sunlight that splintered across it.

"We'll be away in a few minutes. Did you nod off?"

"I must've done." Harold's tongue felt swollen, thick when he spoke. "Jesus! I was well away," he said. He struggled to sit upright. How long had he been asleep?

"Come on." Eddie patted him on the shoulder. "We've a big day ahead of us. We need to make the most of it. It's the last we'll be having."

Eddie's voice sounded oddly cheerful. Harold turned to look round the club. Others too looked as if they must have dozed off, waiting for the coach to arrive. There was a half-awake look to most of them.

"Next stop The Farmer's Glory," the driver said as Harold clambered onto the coach a few minutes later, hauling himself up step by step, using both hands on the handrail. The driver's voice sounded lacklustre. "Full English - for those who can manage it," he ended with a stifled yawn.

Harold hoped he felt better than he looked. The driver's face seemed vacant, half asleep, as if he'd struggled to climb out of bed this morning.

What's wrong with everyone? Only Eddie looked eager and bright. Perhaps they'd drunk too many beers on empty stomachs. It never used to bother him, but he wasn't getting any younger, he thought.

"The last coach trip," Harold murmured as the coach set off.

"You could say that," Eddie responded.

Which was when Harold found himself stumbling through half forgotten memories, of things he thought they'd already done. A hundred-pound win on the last race. He could feel every greasy twenty-pound note the bookie had handed to him between his fingers. He could still taste the overdone steak he'd struggled to chew in the restaurant before they left for the Revellers. Some of the stand-up's jokes echoed through his head, corny, crude, bludgeoned by lips too close to the microphone. And the boy-like singer, crooning something sentimental, he couldn't remember what. He'd been in *The X-Factor*, hadn't he? A semi-finalist? Then the coldness of the coach when they climbed inside…

He looked at Eddie. "You weren't just late; you should never have been there."

Eddie's smile was unwavering.

"What did you do, Eddie? Kill yourself? Take an overdose?"

Which was ridiculous, he knew. The stupidest things he had ever said.

"Some days are just too good to be over," Eddie replied. "Some days should never end."

Somewhere in the back of his mind Harold remembered the pain of glass and metal hitting him, of screams as flames licked through the coach.

As he stared at Eddie his appetite for the Full English ahead of them drained away.

THE SATYR'S HEAD

To turn and look upon its face,
Brought fear I'd never known -
The shadow has ever haunted me,
As I walk the earth so alone -

Karl Edward Wagner

As Henry Lamson looked from the gate of his brother's farm on the outskirts of Pire, he noticed that someone was walking along the lane in his direction. Although it did nothing to disconcert him at the time, he did wonder, as he bid farewell to the silhouetted figures in the doorway, before setting off for his bus stop, why someone should have been coming back from the moors at this time of the night, especially when it had been pouring down with rain all day.

Shrugging his shoulders, Lamson pulled his raincoat collar up high about his neck against the drizzle and picked his way as carefully as he could between the puddles in the deeply rutted lane. He wished now, as his feet sank in the half-hidden mud, that he had thought to bring a torch with him when he came on his visit, since the moon, though full, only faintly showed through the clouds, and the lane was for the most part in shadow.

Engrossed as he was in finding a reasonably dry route along the lane, he did not notice until a few minutes later, when the lights of his brother's farm had disappeared beyond the hedgerow, that the figure he had seen was nearing him quickly. Already he could hear his footsteps along the lane.

Petulantly pausing to disentangle a snapped thorn branch that had caught on his trouser leg, he turned to watch the hunched figure hobbling towards him. A threadbare overcoat of an indeterminate colour swayed from about his body. In one hand he grasped a worn flat cap, while the other was thrust in his overcoat pocket for warmth.

When he finally succeeded in freeing himself of the twig, Lamson made to continue on his way; the man was obviously nothing more than a tramp, and an old one at that. As he started off, though, he heard him call out in a cracked bellow that rose and died in one breath:

"'Arf a mo' there!"

Irritated at the drizzle that was soaking inexorably through his coat, Lamson sighed impatiently. As the tramp hurried towards him through the gloom, he slowly made out his bristly, coarse and wrinkled face, whose dirt-grained contours were glossy with rain.

The old man stumbled to a halt and raucously coughed a volley of phlegm on the ground. The pale grey slime merged with the mud. Lamson watched him wipe his dribbling mouth with the top of his cap. Disgusted at the spectacle, Lamson asked him what the matter was.

"Are you feeling ill?" He hoped that he wasn't. The last thing he wanted was to be burdened with someone like this.

"Ill?" The old man laughed smugly. "Ne'er 'ad a day's illness in my life. Ne'er!"

He coughed and spat more phlegm on the ground. Lamson looked away from it.

Perhaps mistaking the reason for this action, the tramp said: "But I don't want to 'olds you up. I'll walk alon' with you, if you don't mind me doin'. That's all I called you for. It's a lonely place to be by yoursel'. Too lonely, eh?"

Lamson was uncertain whether this was a question or not. Relieved that the man was at least not against continuing down the lane, he nodded curtly and set off, the old man beside him.

"A raw night, to be sure," the old man said, with a throaty chuckle.

Lamson felt a wave of revulsion sweep over him as he glanced at the old man's face in the glimmering light of one of the few lamp posts by the lane. He had never before seen anyone whose flesh gave off such an unnatural look of roughness. Batrachian in some indefinable way, with thick and flaccid lips, a squat nose and deeply sunken eyes, he had the appearance of almost complete depravity. Lamson stared at the seemingly scaly knuckles of his one bare hand.

"Have you come far?" Lamson asked.

"Far?" The man considered the word reflectively. "Not really far, I s'ppose," he conceded, with a further humourless chuckle. "And you," he asked in return, "are you goin' far, or just into Pire?"

Lamson laughed. "Not walking, I'm not. Just on to the bus stop at the end of the lane, where I should just about catch the seven fifty-five for the centre." He looked across at a distant farm amidst the hills about Pire; its tiny windows stood out in the blackness like feeble fireflies through the intervening miles of rain. He glanced at his watch. Another eight minutes and his bus would be due. As he looked up, Lamson was relieved to see the hedgerow end, giving way at a junction to the tarmac road that ran up along the edge of the moors from Fenley. The bus shelter stood beside a dry-stone wall, cemented by Nature with tangled tussocks of grass. Downhill, between the walls and lines of trees, were the pinpointed lines of street lights etched across the valley floor. It was an infallibly awe-inspiring sight, and Lamson felt as if he had passed through the sullen voids of Perdition and regained Life once more.

On reaching the shelter he stepped beneath its corrugated roof out of the rain. Turning around as he nudged a half empty carton of chips to one side he saw that the man was still beside him.

"Are you going into Pire as well"' Lamson asked. He tried, not too successfully, to keep his real feelings out of his voice. Not only did he find the tramp's company in itself distasteful, but there was a fetid smell around him which was reminiscent in some way of sweat and of seaweed rotting on a stagnant beach. It was disturbing in that it brought thoughts, or half thoughts, of an unpleasant type to his mind. Apparently unaware of the effect he was having on Lamson, the tramp was preoccupied in staring back at the moors. Willows and shrubs were thrown back and forth in the gusts, intensifying his feelings of loneliness about the place.

Finally replying to Lamson's inquiry, the tramp said:

"There's nowhere else a body can go, is there? I've got to sleep. An' I can't sleep out in this." His flat, bristly, toad-like head turned around. There was a dim yellow light in his eyes. "I'll find a doss somewhere."

Lamson looked back to see if the bus was in sight, though there were another four minutes to yet go before it was due. The empty expanse of wet tarmac looked peculiarly lonely in the jaundiced light of the sodium lamps along the road.

Fidgeting nervously beside him, the old man seemed to have lost what equanimity he'd had before. Every movement he made seemed to cry out the desire to be on his way once more. It was as if he was morbidly afraid of something on the moors behind him.

Lamson was bewildered. What could there be on the moors to worry him? Yet, whether there was really something there for him to worry about or not, there was no mistaking the relief which he showed when they at last heard the whining roar of the double-decker from Fenley turning the last bend in the slope uphill, its headlights silhouetting the bristling shrubs along the road and glistening the droplets of rain. A moment later it drew up before them, comfortingly bright against the ice-grey hills and sky. Climbing on board, Lamson sat down beside the nearest window, rubbing a circle in the misted glass to look outside.

He was dismayed when the tramp slumped down beside him. In the smoke-staled air the smell around the old man became even more noticeable than before, whilst his cold, damp body seemed to cut him off from the warmth he had welcomed on boarding the bus.

Apparently unconcerned by such matters, the tramp grinned sagaciously, saying that it was good to be moving once more. His spirits were blatantly rising, and he ceased looking back at the moors after a couple of minutes, seemingly satisfied.

In an effort to ignore the fetor exuded by the man, Lamson concentrated on looking out of the window, watching the trees and meadows pass by as they progressed into Pire, till they were supplanted by the gardened houses of the suburbs.

"'Ave you a light?" The frayed stub of a cigarette was stuck between the tramp's horny fingers.

His lips drawn tight in annoyance, Lamson turned around to face him as he searched through his pockets. Was there to be no end to his intolerable bother? he wondered. His eyes strayed unwillingly about the scaly knuckles of the man's hand, to the grimily web-like flaps of skin stretched at their joints. It was a disgustingly malformed object, and Lamson was certain that he had never before seen anyone whose every aspect excited nothing so much as sheer nausea.

Producing a box of matches, he struck one for him, then waited while he slowly sucked life into his cigarette.

When he settled back a moment later, the tramp brought the large hand he had kept thrust deep in his overcoat pocket out and held it clenched before Lamson.

"Ever seen anythin' like this afore?" he asked cryptically. Like the withered petals of a grotesque orchid, his fingers uncurled from the palm of his hand.

Prepared as he was for some forgotten medal from the War, tarnished and grimy, with a caterpillar segment of wrinkled ribbon attached, Lamson was surprised when he saw instead a small but well-carved head of dull black stone, which looked as though it might have been broken from a statue about three feet or so in height.

Lamson looked at the tramp as the bus trundled to a momentary stop and two boisterous couples on a night out climbed on board, laughing and giggling at some murmured remark. Oblivious of them, Lamson let the tramp place the object in his hand. Though he was attracted by it, he was simultaneously and inexplicably repelled. There was a certain hungry look to the man's face on the broken head which seemed to go further than that of mere hunger for food.

Lamson turned the head about in his fingers, savoring the pleasant, soap-like surface of the stone.

"A strange thing to find out there, you'd think, wouldn't you?" the old man said, pointing his thick black stub of a thumb back at the moors.

"So you found it out there?" Somehow there was just enough self control in Lamson's voice to rob it of its disbelief. Though he would have wanted nothing more a few minutes earlier than to be rid of the man, he felt a yearning now to own the head himself that deterred him from insulting the tramp. After all, there was surely no other reason for the man showing the thing to him except to sell it. And although he had never before felt any intense fascination in archaeology, there was something about the head which made Lamson desire it now. He was curious about it as a small boy is curious about a toy he has seen in a shop window.

Intent on adding whatever gloss of credibility to his tale that he could, the old tramp continued, saying:

"It were in a brook. I found it by chance as I were gettin' m'self some water for a brew. It'd make a nice paperweight, I thought. I thought so as soon as I saw it. It'd make a nice paperweight, I thought." He laughed self-indulgently, wiping his mouth with the sleeve of his coat. "But I've no paper to put it on."

Lamson looked down at the carving and smiled.

*

When the bus drew up at the terminus, Lamson was surprised, though not dismayed, when the tramp hurriedly climbed off and merged with the passing crowds outside. His bowlegged gait and crookedly unkempt figure were too suggestive of sickness and deformity for Lamson's tastes, and he felt more eager than ever for a salutary pint of beer in a pub before going on home to his flat.

Pressing his way through the queues outside the Cinerama

on Market Street, he made for the White Bull, whose opaque doors swung open before him with an out blowing bubble of warm, beery air.

One drink later, and another in hand, he stepped across to a vacant table up in a corner of the lounge, placing his glass beside screwed-up bag of crisps.

A group of men were arguing amongst themselves nearby, one telling another, as of someone giving advice:

"A standing prick has no conscience."

There was a nodding of heads and another affirmed: "That's true enough."

Disregarding them as they sorted out what they were having for their next round of drinks, Lamson reached in his pocket and brought out the head. A voice on the television fixed above the bar said:

"You can be a Scottish nationalist or a Welsh nationalist and no one says anything about it, but as soon as you say you're a British nationalist, everyone starts calling out 'Fascist!'"

Two of the men nodded to each other in agreement.

Holding the head in the palm of his hand, Lamson realized for the first time just how heavy it was. If not for the broken neck, which showed clearly enough that it was made out of stone, he would have thought it to have been molded from lead. As he peered at it, he noticed that there were two small ridges on its brows which looked as though they had once been horns

As he studied them, he felt that if they had remained in their entirety, the head would have looked almost satiric, despite the bloated lips. In fact, the slightly raised eyebrows and long, straight nose - or what remained of them - were still reminiscent of Pan.

He heard a glass being placed on the table beside him. When he looked up he saw that it was Allan Sutcliffe.

"I didn't notice you in here before. Have you only just got in?" Lamson asked.

Sutcliffe wiped his rain-spotted glasses on a handkerchief as he sat down, nodding his head. He replaced his glasses, then thirstily drank down a third of his pint before unbuttoning his raincoat and loosening the scarf about his neck. His face was flushed as if he had been running.

"I didn't think I'd be able to get here in time for a drink. I have to be off again soon to get to the Film Society. What have you got there, Henry? You been digging out your garden or something?"

Almost instinctively, Lamson cupped his hands about the head.

"It'd be strange sort of garden in a second floor flat, wouldn't it?" he replied acidly.

He drew his hands in towards his body, covering what little still showed of the head with the ends of his scarf. Somehow he felt ashamed of the thing, almost as if it was obscene and repulsive and peculiarly shameful.

"Where did you say you were off to?" he asked, intending to change the subject. "The Film Society? What are they presenting tonight?"

"*Nosferatu*. The original. Why? D'you fancy coming along to it as well? It's something of a classic, I believe. Should be good."

Lamson shook his head.

"Sorry, but I don't feel up to it tonight. I only stopped in for a pint or two before going on home and getting an early night. I've had a long day already, what with helping my brother, Peter, redecorating the inside of his farmhouse. I'm about done in."

Glancing significantly at the clock above the bar, Sutcliffe drained his glass, saying, as he placed it back on the table afterwards: "I'll have to be off now. It starts in another ten minutes."

"I'll see you tomorrow as we planned," Lamson said. "At twelve, if that's still okay?"

Sutcliffe nodded as he stood up to go.

"We'll meet at the Wimpy, then I can get a bite to eat before we set off for the match."

"Okay."

As Sutcliffe left, Lamson opened his sweat softened hands and looked at the head concealed in the cramped shadows in between. Now that his friend had gone, he felt puzzled at his reaction with the thing. What was it about the thing that should affect him like this? he wondered to himself. Placing it back in his pocket, he decided that he had had enough of the pub and strode outside, buttoning his coat against the rain.

*

Sunlight poured with a cold liquidity through his bedroom window when Lamson awoke. It shone across the cellophane that protected the spines of the hardbound books on the shelves facing his bed, obscuring their titles. It seemed glossy and bright and clean, with the freshness of newly fallen snow.

Yawning contentedly, he stretched, then drew his dressing gown onto his shoulders as he gazed out of the window. Visible beyond the roof opposite was a bright and cloudless sky. He felt the last dull dregs of sleep sloughing from him as he rubbed the fine granules that had collected in his eyes away. Somewhere he could hear a radio playing a light pop tune, though it was almost too faint to make out.

Halfway through washing he remembered the dreams. They had completely passed from his mind on wakening, and it was with an unpleasant shudder that they returned to him now.

The veneer of his cheerfulness was dulled by the recollection, and he paused in his ablutions to look back at his bed. They were dreams he was not normally troubled with, and he was loathe to think of them now.

"To Hell with them!" he muttered self-consciously as he returned to scrubbing the threads of dirt from underneath his nails.

*

The measured chimes of the clock on the neo-Gothic tower, facing him across the neat churchyard of St. James, were tolling midday when Lamson walked past the Municipal Library. Sutcliffe, who worked at a nearby firm of accountants as an articled clerk, would be arriving at the Wimpy further along the street any time now. Going inside, Lamson ordered himself a coffee and took a seat by the window. Absent-mindedly, he scratched his hand, wondering nonchalantly, when he noticed what he was doing, if he had accidentally brushed it against some of the nettles that grew up against the churchyard wall. A few minutes later Sutcliffe arrived, and the irritation passed from his mind, forgotten.

"You're looking a bit bleary eyed today, Henry," Sutcliffe remarked cheerfully. "An early night, indeed! Too much bed and not enough sleep, that's your trouble."

"I wish it was," Lamson replied. "I slept well enough last night. Too well, perhaps."

"Come again?"

"Some dreams -" Lamson started to explain, before he was interrupted by Sutcliffe as the waitress arrived.

"Wimpy and chips and coffee, please."

When she'd gone, Sutcliffe said: "I'm sorry. What was that you were saying?"

But the inclination to tell him had gone. Instead, Lamson talked about the Rovers' chances this afternoon in their match against Rochdale. As they spoke, though, his mind was not wholly on what they were talking about. He was troubled, though he did not know properly why, by the dreams he had been about to tell Sutcliffe about, but which, on reconsideration, he had decided to keep to himself.

He was glad that he had a full day ahead of him, what with the football match this afternoon and a date with Joan at the Tavern tonight. Sutcliffe was taking his fiancé with them, and it promised to be an enjoyable evening for them all. He only wished that his relationship with Joan, who he had been going out with now for three months, wasn't so peculiarly Platonic.

142

Whether this was his fault or hers, he did not know. A bit of both, he supposed, when he thought about it. Yet, if things did not improve very soon, he knew that their relationship, whatever his own inner feelings might be, would start to cool. Was this the cause of the dreams? he wondered, as he tried to concentrate on what Sutcliffe was saying. There did not seem to be any other reason he could think of at the moment that could account for them, and he decided that this must be it.

*

As Lamson walked home through the vaporous gloom beneath the old street lamps along Beechwood Avenue, after leaving Joan at her parents' home, his mind was deep in thought. It had been, as he had expected, an enjoyable evening, but only because of the new folk group they had been able to listen to at the Tavern. Joan had been no different than before: friendly and feminine in every way that he could wish, talkative - but not too much so - intelligent, amusing, and yet... and yet what was missing? Or was it him? What was it, he wondered, that made him feel so fatherly towards her, instead of the way in which at all other times he wished, even yearned, to be?

If not for the unexpected sound of someone slipping on the pavement some distance behind him, he would not have been brought out of his reverie until he reached Station Road and the last, short stretch to his flat. As it was, he half intentionally, half instinctively turned around to see if someone had fallen.

But all he glimpsed on the otherwise deserted avenue was the vague impression of someone merging hurriedly with the shadowy privet bushes midway between the feeble light of the lamp posts further back. So fleeting was the impression, though, that he would have taken it for the blurred motion of a cat that had raced across the avenue, but for the distinct recollection of something having slipped on the footpath.

For a moment or two he waited and watched in vain, certain that whoever or whatever hid in the gloom of the privets had not moved since he turned and was only waiting for him to turn back again to emerge. It was disturbing, and he tried to play down his nervousness with the thought that it was probably only some kids playing an idiotic game of hide and seek in the dark. Unconvinced though he was by this explanation, it was substantial enough for him as an excuse to turn around with at least the pretense of indifference and continue on his way home. Even so, it was with a definite feeling of relief, however, when he reached Station Road, where the bright shop windows, neon signs and the passing cars and buses brought him back into reality. With more speed than he usually employed he strode along to the door leading into his flat and raced up the two flights of stairs to his rooms.

As he closed the door behind him, he noticed the small black head he had bought from the tramp perched where he had left it on the dresser, its outline gleaming in the reflection of the street lights outside.

It was looking towards him, crooked at an obtuse angle on its broken neck. He threw his overcoat onto the bed and stepped to the window to draw the curtains together before switching on the light. He felt at the radiator opposite his bed by the bookcase. It was just lukewarm.

As he stared morosely about the room, he wondered what had made him buy the head. What perverse attraction had struck him about it before had gone, and all he could see in it now was ugliness and decay. He picked it up. It wasn't as if he could legitimately claim he'd bought it out of some kind of archaeological interest. It was years since he'd last pottered in that subject at school, and what enthusiasm he may have once had for it had been lost to him long ago. For a moment he rubbed the small lumps on its brows, but he felt too tired suddenly to study it tonight. There was a nagging ache in his back and his arms felt stiff, while the rash-like irritation had returned to tingle on the back of his hands.

Lamson dropped the stone head back on the dresser and began to change into his pajamas. He felt too tired now to think or even place his clothes folded up, as he normally did, on the table beside his bed.

For a moment he struggled to keep awake, but he could not resist. He did not want to resist. All he wanted to do was to surrender himself, his body and soul, to the dull black nothingness of sleep.

Sleep quickly overcame him as he lay on his bed and closed his eyes.

And in his sleep, he dreamed.

There was a wood in his dream, a great, deep, darkly mysterious wood that filled him with unease as he listened to its decrepit oaks groaning in the wind.

He stood before it alone. But he did not feel alone. He could sense something watching him malevolently from the gloomy depths of the wood.

The twilight passed into the darkness of night. Shadows glided silently through the trees, gathering as if to stare out at him with small, round, rubicund eyes. Or was it his own eyes playing tricks with the dark?

Then he saw something emerge from the waist high ferns, crawling on all fours across the ground. It was almost black, its naked flesh dry and coarse, strung tight about its jutting bones. Its legs, though hairless, were as the legs of a goat, whilst shrunken breasts, some twelve in number, hung limply from its chest. They swayed as it moved, its jaundiced eyes gleaming from the deep black depths of their sockets with a foul anticipation. There was a convulsive twitching in its long, thin, bony hands.

Unable to move, Lamson watched it crawl towards him. Its penis was hard with lust, the dark nipples of its breasts enlarged and tight. Its lips were wet with overflowing saliva as it drew towards him.

Though partially human, it was hideously inhuman, a foul, unearthly, cacodaemoniacal Pan. Stiff black horns curved upwards from its brows; a scaled and rat-like tail flicked from its spine. He could see the mounting tension of its poised phallus.

145

He tried to scream.

With all his strength he tried to scream, to cry out and tear himself away from the hideous creature creeping towards him, but there was nothing he could do. He was paralyzed and defenseless.

A murmured chanting sibilantly issued encircling trees, flitting with the wind.

"*Ma dheantar aon scriosadh, athru, gearradh, lot no milleadh ar an ordu feadfar diultu d'e a ioc.*"

The rhythmic chanting began to mimic the frenzied beating of a heart, faster and deeper, as the satyr, swaying its lean torso to the rhythms of the chants, came upon Lamson. Its left hand grasped him about the thigh, pulling him down till he knelt on the ground. Its fetid breath blew hot into his face like the searing gusts of a newly opened furnace. He could see the wrinkles in its clammy flesh and the sores suppurating on its lips.

With renewed urgency he wrenched himself free and tried to roll out of its way across the grass. But before he even saw it move, he felt its hands grasping him once more. He kicked out at it, whimpering. Its talons tore a deep gash in his trousers and its palm slid searchingly down his leg.

Once more he kicked.

With a slow deliberation it reached out for the buckle of his belt and ripped it free.

It was crouched over him, its softly repulsive underbelly almost touching his legs. In the feeble light its body seemed huge.

With a sudden exertion Lamson managed at last to emit a scream.

As its hand reached for him between his legs darkness sprang up about him like a monstrous whirlpool.

He felt dizzy and sick, shuddering with horror as he awoke, his body drenched with perspiration in the tangled blankets of his bed. At the same time, he felt the final climax of an orgasm clasp hold of him.

He lay back and gasped, weak with the intensity of his ejaculation. He felt suddenly fouled, as if he'd been dragged through demoniacal cesspools of sin.

Nauseated, he looked across from his bed at the carving. Its coarse features seemed even more hideous to him now than before, and he did not doubt but that in some repulsively Freudian way its lecherous features - mirrored, as he now realized, on the demon creature of his nightmare - had influenced his sleeping mind. As he looked at it he found it difficult to understand how he had failed to notice the unclean lust rampant about its face before, like some infernal incubus roused by the harlots of Hell. As he washed himself clean a few minutes later he wondered if it would not be better to get rid of the head, to throw it away and forget it, and in doing so, hopefully, rid himself of the dreams.

Only once, while he dressed, did a discordant thought make him wonder if, perhaps, the dream wasn't connected in some way with his unsatisfactory relationship with Joan. But the two things were at such extremes in his mind that he could not connect them with anything other than shame. As he looked at the stone this shame transferred itself to this object, intensifying into a firm resolve to get rid of the thing. How could he possibly make any kind of headway with Joan, he told himself, with such a foul obscenity as that thing troubling him?

When Lamson left his flat a short time later, carrying the head in his raincoat pocket, it was with steps so unsteady that he wondered if he was coming down with something. The irritation on his hands had, if anything, become even worse, while aches and pains announced their presence from all over his body while he walked. He wondered if he had overstrained himself when he was helping his brother redecorate his farm, though he'd felt fit enough the day before. The Sunday morning streets were agreeably deserted as he walked along them. The only cars in sight were parked by the kerb. In a way he was glad that the dream had woken him as early as it had. Just past eight thirty now, it would be a while yet, he knew, before the city would start stirring into life today.

"Dirt-y o-old ma-an, dirty o-old ma-an!" He looked across to where the singsong voices came from. Two small boys of about ten or eleven years in age, perhaps less, were stood at the corner of the street in a shop doorway. Cheeky little brats, Lamson thought to himself as he noticed the shuffling figure their jeers were directed against, a stooped old man slowly making his way down a street leading off from the main road past a line of overfilled dustbins.

Although Lamson could not see his face he could tell that the old man knew the boys were calling out at him. Slow though his pace was, it was also unmistakably hurried, as if he was trying to get out of their way as quickly as he could on his old, decrepit legs.

"Clear off!" Lamson shouted angrily, feeling sorry for the old man.

The kids yelped and ran off down, laughing.

If he had not felt so weary himself, he would have run after them. How could they act so callously? He watched the old man as he continued up the street. There was something about the painful stoop of his back and the way his legs were bent, that struck a chord of remembrance somewhere. He could almost have been the tramp he met on the moors, except that he hadn't been anything like as decrepit as this man obviously was, not unless his health had failed disastrously over the last couple of days.

Lamson crossed the road and headed up past St. James church, putting the old man out of his mind. The pleasant singing of the birds in the elms that filled the churchyard helped to ease his spirits, and he breathed in the scent of the grass with a genuine feeling of pleasure. He only wished that his legs didn't feel so stiff and tired. He wondered again if he was coming down with a bug of some kind.

He paused suddenly by the wall and felt in his pocket, his fingers moving speculatively about the small stone head. Though he did not know properly why, he decided that the churchyard was too near his flat for him to get rid of the stone here. It would be better if he made his way to the canal where he could lose it properly without trace.

As he turned around to leave, he noticed a slight movement out of the corner of his eye. With a feeling of trepidation, he paused, turned round and anxiously scanned the solemn rows of headstones.

Nothing moved, except for a light film of drizzle that began to filter down through the overhanging boughs of the trees. Yet, even though he could not see anything to account for what he seemed to have glimpsed, like a blurred shadow moving on the edge of his sight, he was sure that he was not mistaken. He stepped up the street to where a narrow gate led into the churchyard. He looked across it once again, and wished that he could make himself leave this suddenly disturbing place, but he could not. With slow, but far from resolute steps, he walked down the asphalt path between the headstones, his senses attuned to the least disturbance about him: the cold moisture of the drizzle on his hands and face, the hissing of the leaves as the rain passed through them, the singing of the birds that echoed and reechoed about him, and the distant murmur of a car along Station Road as the clock tolled a quarter to nine. The air seemed strangely still. Or was it his own overwrought imagination, keyed up by the horrendous nightmare, scenes from which still flickered uncomfortably in front of him? He felt a fluttering sensation in his stomach as he looked along the roughhewn stones of the church with its incised windows of stained glass.

Quickening his pace, as the drizzle began to fall with more weight, he passed round the church. As he walked by the trees on the far side of the building, where they screened it off from the bleak back walls of a derelict mill, he again noticed something move. Was it a dog? he wondered, though it had seemed a little large. He whistled, though there was no response other than a thin, frail echo.

He strode between rows of ornate monuments of polished marble. Was that someone there, crouched in the bushes?

149

"Excuse me!" he called enquiringly. Then stopped. Calling out to a dog, indeed! he thought as he glimpsed what he took to be a large black hound - perhaps an Irish wolf hound - scutter off out of sight between the trees.

As he walked back to the street, he decided that it was about time he got on his way to the canal before the rain got any worse.

The rain did worsen. By the time he reached the towpath of the canal, he was beginning to regret having come out on a morning like this on such a pointless exercise. The rain covered the fields on either side of the canal in a dull grey veil. What colors there were had been reduced to such a washed-out monochrome that the scene reminded him of that in an old and faded photograph. Facing him across the dingy waters of the canal were rows of little sheds and barbed wire fences. Crates of neglected rubbish had been abandoned in the sparsely grassed fields, together with the tyreless carcasses of deserted cars. The fields rose up to the back of a grim row of tenements whose haphazard rooftops formed a jagged black line against the sky. Only the moldering wood of the derelict mills and their soot-grimed bricks on his side of the canal stood out with any clarity.

A dead cat floated in a ring of scum in the stagnant water at his feet, its jellied eyes sightlessly staring at the sky with a dank luminescence.

As he took the stone head from his pocket, Lamson heard someone move behind him. Having thought that he was safely alone, he spun round in surprise.

Crouched deep in the shadows between the walls of the mill, where a gate had once stood, was a man. A long, unbuttoned overcoat hung from about his hunched body. It was a coat that Lamson recognized instantly.

"So it was those kids were shouting at," Lamson accused, as the tramp tottered out into the light. "Have you been following me?" he asked. But there was no response, other than a slight twitching of the old man's blistered lips into what he took to be a smile, though one that was distinctively malignant and sly. "You were following me last night. Weren't you?" Lamson went on. "I heard you when you slipped, so there's no point denying it. And I saw you this morning when those kids were having a go at you. I thought they were being cruel when they shouted out at you, but I don't know now. Perhaps they were right. Perhaps you are a dirty old man, a dirty, insidious and evil old man." Even now there was no more response from the tramp than that same repugnant smile. "Haven't you got a tongue?" Lamson snapped. "Grinning there like a Gargoyle. Well? You were talkative enough when we met on the moors. Have you taken vows of silence since then? Come on! Speak up, damn you!" He clenched his fists, fighting back the impulse to hit him in the face, even though it was almost too strong to resist. What an ugly old creature he was, what with his pockmarked face all rubbery and grey and wet, and those bloated, repulsive lips. A thin, grey trickle of saliva hung down from a corner of his mouth. There was a streak of blood in it. As he stared at him he realized that he looked far worse, far, far worse than before, as if whatever disease had already swollen and eroded his features had suddenly accelerated its effect.

The tramp stared down at the in Lamson's hand.

"Were you after gettin' rid of it? Is that why you've come to this place?" he asked finally.

"Since it's mine, I have every right to, if that's what I want to do," Lamson said, taken aback at the accusation.

"An' why should you choose to do such a thing, I wonder? You liked it enough when I first showed it to you on the bus. Couldn't 'ardly wait to buy it off o' me then, could you? 'Ere's the money, give us the stone, quick as a flash! Couldn't 'ardly wait, you couldn't. An' ere you are, all 'et up an' nervous, can't 'ardly wait to get rid o' the thing. What's the poor sod been doin' to you? Givin' you nightmares, 'as it?"

"What do you mean?"

"What should I mean? Just a joke. That's all. Can't you tell? Ha, ha, ha!" He spat a string of phlegm on the ground. "Only a joke," he went on, wiping his mouth with his sleeve.

"Only a joke, was it?" Lamson asked, his anger inflamed

with indignation at the old man's ill-concealed contempt for him. "And I suppose it was only a joke when you followed me here as well? Or did you have some other purpose in mind? Did you?"

"P'raps I was only tryin' to make sure you came to no 'arm. Wouldn't want no 'arm to come to you now, would I? After all, you bought that 'ead off o' me fair an' square, didn't you? Though it does seem an awful shame to me to toss it into the canal there. Awful shame it'd be. Where'd you get another bit o' stone like that? It's unique, you know, that's what it is right enough. Unique. Wouldn't want to throw it into no canal, would you? Where's the sense in it? Or the use? Could understand if there was somethin' bad an' nasty about it. Somethin' unpleasant, like. But what's bad an' nasty about that? Don't give you no nightmares, now, does it? Nothin' like that? Course not! Little bit o' stone like that? An' yet, 'ere you are, all 'et up an' ready to toss it away, an' no reason to it. I can't understand it at all. I can't. I swear it." He shook his head reproachfully, though there was a cunning grin about his misshapen mouth, as if laughing at a secret joke. "Throwin' it away," he went on in the same infuriatingly mocking voice, "Ne'er would ha' thought o' doin' such a thing - old bit o' stone like that. You know 'ow much it might be worth? Can you even guess? Course not! An' yet you get it for next to nothin' off o' me, only keep it for a day or so, then the next thing I knows, 'ere you are all ready to toss it like an empty can into the canal. An' that's what you've come 'ere for, isn't it?"

"And if it is, why are you here?" Lamson asked angrily. The old man knew too much - far, far too much. It wasn't natural! "What are you?" he asked. "And why have you been spying on me? Come on, give me an answer!"

"An answer, is it? Well, p'raps I will. It's too late now, I can tell, for me to do any 'arm in lettin' you know. 'E's 'ad 'Is 'ands on you by now, no doubt, Eh?"

Lamson felt a stirring in his loins as he remembered the dream he had woken from barely two hours ago. But the old man couldn't mean that. It was impossible for him to know about it, utterly, completely, irrefutably impossible! Lamson tried to make himself leave, but he couldn't, not until he had heard what the old man had to say, even though he knew that he didn't want to listen. He had no choice. He couldn't. "Are you going to answer my questions?" he asked, his voice sounding far firmer than he felt.

The tramp leered disgustedly.

"'Aven't 'ad enough, 'ave you? Want to 'ear about it as well?"

"As well as what?"

The tramp laughed.

"You know. Though you pretend that you don't, you know all right. You know." He wiped one watering, red-rimmed eye. "I 'spect you'll please 'Im a might bit better 'n' me. For a while, at least. I wasn't much for 'Im, even at the first. Too old. Too sick. Even then I was too sick. Sicker now, though, o' course. But that's 'ow it is. That's 'ow it's got to be, I s'ppose. 'E wears you out. That 'E does. Wears you out. But you, now, you, you're as young as 'E could ask for. An' fit. Should last a while. A long, long while, I think, before 'E wears you out. Careful! Wouldn't want to drop 'Im now, would you?"

It seemed as if something cold and clammy was clenching itself like some tumorous hand inside him. With a shudder of revulsion, Lamson looked down at the stone in his hand. Was he mistaken or was there a look of satisfaction on its damnable face? He stared at it hard, feeling himself give way to a nauseating fear that drained his limbs of their strength.

"I thought you were o' the right sort for 'Im when I saw you on that lane," the tramp said. "I'm ne'er wrong 'bout things like that."

As if from a great distance Lamson heard himself ask what he meant.

"Right sort? What the fucking hell do you mean: the right sort?"

"Should ha' thought you'd know," he replied, touching him on the hand with his withered fingers.

Lamson jerked his hand away.

"You dirty old sod!" he snapped, fear and disgust adding tension to his voice. "You - you..." He did not want to face the things hinted at. He didn't! They were lies, all lies, nothing but lies! With a sudden cry of half-hearted annoyance, both at the tramp and at himself for his weakness, he pushed past and ran back along the towpath. He ran as the rain began to fall with more force and the sky darkened overhead. He ran as the city began to come to life and church bells tolled their beckoning chimes for the first services of the day.

*

"I can't understand you," Sutcliffe said as he collected a couple of pints from the bar and brought them back to their table by the door. "Excuse me," he added, as he pushed his chair between a pair of outstretched legs from the next table. "Right - Thanks."

Loosening his scarf, he sat down with a shake of his tousled head.

"Like the Black Hole of Calcutta in here," he said. He took a sip of his pint, watching Lamson as he did so. His friend's face looked so pale and lifeless these days, its unhealthiness emphasized by the dark sores that had erupted about his mouth.

"In what way can't you understand me?" Lamson asked.

There was a dispirited tiredness to his voice which Sutcliffe could tell didn't spring from boredom or disinterest.

Folding his arms, Sutcliffe leant over the table towards him.

"It's two weeks now since you last went out with Joan. And that was the night we all went to the Tavern. Since then nothing. No word or anything. From you... But Joan has called round to your flat four times this week, though you weren't apparently in. Unless you've found someone else, you'd better know that she won't keep on waiting for you to see her. She has her pride, and she can tell when she's being snubbed. Don't get me wrong. I wouldn't like you to think I'm interfering, but it was Joan who asked me to mention this to you if I should bump into you. So, if you have some reason for avoiding her, I'd be glad if you'd let me know." He shrugged, slightly embarrassed by what he'd had to say. "If you'd prefer to tell me to mind my own bloody business I'd understand, of course. But, even if only for Joan's sake, I'd rather you'd say something."

Suppressing a cough, Lamson wiped his mouth with a handkerchief, held ready in his hand. He wished he could tell Sutcliffe the reason why he was avoiding Joan, for a deliberate avoidance it was.

"I haven't been feeling too good recently," he replied evasively.

"Is it anything serious?"

Lamson shook his head. "No, it's nothing serious. I'll be better in a while. A bad dose of flu, that's all. But it's been lingering on."

Sutcliffe frowned. He did not like the way in which his friend was acting these days, so unlike the open and friendly manner in which he had always behaved before, at least with him. Even allowing for flu, this neither explained the change in his character nor the peculiar swellings about his mouth. If it was flu, it was flu of a far more serious nature than any he'd ever had himself. And how, for Christ' s sake, could that explain the way in which his skin seemed to have become coarse and dry, especially about the knuckles on his hands?

"Have you been eating the right kinds of foods?" Sutcliffe asked. "I know what it can be like living in a flat. Tried it once for a while. Never again! Give me a boarding house anytime. Too much like hard work for me to cook my own meals, I can tell you. I dare say you find it much like that yourself."

"A little," Lamson admitted, staring at his beer without interest or appetite as three men wearing election rosettes pressed by towards the bar. One of them said:

"I wouldn't be at all surprised if it wasn't something all these Asians have been bringing into the country. There's been an increase in TB already, and that was almost unheard of a few years ago."

"It's certainly like nothing I've ever heard of, that's for sure," one of the other two said.

As the men waited for their drinks, one of them turned around, smiling in recognition when he saw Lamson.

"Hello there. I didn't notice you were here when we came in."

"Still working hard, I see," Lamson said, nodding at the red, white and blue National Front rosette on the man's jacket.

"No rest for the wicked. Someone's got to do the Devil's work," the man joked as the other two smiled in appreciation of his joke. "It's the local elections in another fortnight," he added.

Collecting their drinks, the men sat down at the table beside Lamson and Sutcliffe.

"I overheard you talking about TB. Has there been a sudden outbreak or something?" Lamson asked.

"Not TB," the man said. "We've just been talking to an old woman who told us that a tramp was found dead in an alleyway near her house earlier this week. From what we were able to gather from her, even the ambulance men themselves, who you'd think would be pretty well-hardened to that kind of thing, were shaken by what they saw."

"What was it'" Sutcliffe asked. "A mugging?"

"No," Reynolds - the man who had spoken - said with a dull satisfaction. "Apparently he died from some kind of disease. They're obviously trying to keep news about it down, though we're going to try to find out what we can about it. So far there's been no mention in the press, though the local rag - *Billy's Weekly Liar* - isn't acting out of character there, especially with the elections coming up. So, just what it is we don't know, though it must be serious. Sickening is how the old woman described him, though how she got a look at him is anybody's guess. But you know what these old women are like. Somehow or other she managed to get a bloody good look - too good a look, I think, for her own peace of mind in the end! According to what she told us there were swellings and sores and discolourations all over his body. And blood dripping out of his mouth, as if his insides had been eaten away."

Lamson shuddered, though he knew the man was probably exaggerating. He didn't give much credence to most of what he said. He'd always been a bit dodgy – and seemed even dodgier now that he had become involved in politics.

"What's the matter?" Sutcliffe asked as he lit a cigarette.

Lamson smiled weakly.

"Just someone stepping over my grave, that's all," he said. He took a long drink of his beer as the three men drained theirs. Putting his glass down, empty, Reynolds stood up. "We'd better be off back to our canvassing or someone'll be doing a clog dance on our graves. And we'll be in them!"

As the men left, Lamson said that he could do with a whisky.

"Just because of what you heard about some poor old sod of a tramp?" Sutcliffe asked. "I wouldn't take much notice of Reynolds. The man's a clown."

"It's not the old tramp," Lamson said. "God help his miserable soul; he was probably better off dead anyway" Though what he said was meant to sound offhand, his voice lacked the lightness of tone to carry it off successfully. Realizing this, he pushed his glass away. "I'm sorry - I must seem like poor company tonight. I think it would perhaps be better if I set off home. Perhaps we'll meet up again tomorrow night? Yes?"

"If you say so," Sutcliffe replied amicably. "You do look a bit under the weather tonight." A Hell of a lot under the weather, he added silently to himself. "Anyhow, now that you mention it, it's about time I was on my way as well. I'll walk along with you to my bus stop. It's on your way."

As they stepped out of the pub, Sutcliffe asked if he had been sleeping well recently.

"What makes you ask?"

"Your eyes," Sutcliffe said as the wind pushed against them, a torn newspaper scuttering along the gutter. "Red-rimmed and bleary. You ought to get a few early nights. Or see if your doctor can prescribe some sleeping pills for you. It's probably what you need."

Lamson stared down the road as they walked along it. How

cold and lonely it looked, even with the cars hissing by through puddles of rain, and the people walking hurriedly along the pavement. There was a smell of fish and chips and the pungent aroma of curry as they passed a takeaway, but even this failed to make him feel at home on the street. He felt foreign and lost, alienated to the things and places which had previously seemed so familiar to him. Even with Sutcliffe he felt almost alone, sealed within himself.

As they parted a few minutes later at Sutcliffe's stop outside the Unit Four on Market Street, his friend said:

"I'll be expecting you tomorrow. You've been keeping far too much to yourself recently. If you don't watch out, you'll end up a hermit, and that's no kind of fate for a friend of mine. So mind you're ready when I call round. Okay?"

Lamson said that he would be. There was no point in trying to evade him. Sutcliffe was too persistent for that. Nor did he really want to evade him, not deep down. He pulled his coat collar up high about his neck and started off purposefully for his flat.

*

There was a gloom to his bedroom which came from more than just an absence of light, since even during the day it was there. It was a gloom which seemed to permeate everything within it like a spreading stain. As soon as Lamson stepped inside he was aware of the gloom, in which even the newest of his possessions seemed faded and cheap.

He looked at the stone head.

It drew his attention almost compulsively. Of everything it was the only object in the room that had not been affected by this strange malaise. Was it gloating? he wondered. Gloating at the way in which it had triumphed over everything else in the flat, including (or especially) the framed photo of Joan, with her blond hair curled so characteristically about her face? You're trapped with me, it seemed to say like some grotesque spider

158

that had caught him on its dusty web, its repulsively hybrid goatlike features smirking and sneering. Lamson rubbed his hands together vigorously, trying to push the thoughts out of his mind. I must get rid of the thing, he told himself (as he had continually done, though without result, for the past two weeks).

He glanced at his unmade bed with distaste and a feeling of shame.

"Oh, God," he whispered self-consciously, "if could get rid of the obsession. Because that is all it is. No more. Only an obsession, which I can and must somehow forget." Or was it? There was no way in which he could get away from the doubt. After all, he thought, how could he satisfactorily explain the way in which the tramp had seemed able to read his thoughts and know just what it was that he'd dreamed? Or was he only a part of this same single-minded and delusive obsession? he wondered, somewhat hopefully, as his mind grew dull with tiredness. He glanced at his watch. How much longer could he fight against falling asleep? One hour? Two? Eventually, though, he would have to give in. It was one fight, as he so well knew by now, which no one could win, no matter how much they might want to, or with how much will.

In an effort to concentrate his thoughts he picked out a book from the shelf randomly. It was *Over the Bridge* by Richard Church. He had quite enjoyed reading it once several months ago, but the words did not seem to have any substance in his brain anymore. Letters, like melting figures of ice, lost form and swam and merged as if the ink was still wet and slowly soaking through the pages as he watched.

When, as was inevitable, he finally lost consciousness and slept, he became aware of a change in the atmosphere. There was a warmth which seemed womb-like and wrong in the open air. It disturbed him as he looked up at the stars prickling the sky, the deep, black, canopied darkness of the sky.

On every side trees rose from the gloom, their boughs bent over like thousands upon thousands of enormous, extended fingers, black in their damp decay. Their leaves were like limpets, pearly and wet, as they shivered in the rising winds.

Before him a glade led down beneath the trees.

Undecided as to which way he should go, Lamson looked about himself uncertainly, hoping for a sign, for some indication - however faint or elusive - as to which path was the one he should take. There seemed to be so many of them, leading like partially erased pencil lines across a grimy sheet of paper through the over-luxuriant grass. Somewhere there was a sound, though it was so dimmed and distorted by the distance separating him from its source. Sibilantly, vaguely, the rhythmic words wound their ways between the trees.

Finding himself miming them, he turned his back to the sounds and started for the glade. Even as he moved he knew that he had made a mistake. But he knew, also, with a sudden, wild wrenching of his heart, that there was no escape. Not now. It was something which he knew had either happened before or was preordained, that no matter what he did there was no way in which he could escape from what was going to happen next. He felt damned - by God, the Devil and himself.

Crest fallen, as the awfulness of what he knew was about to happen next came over him, he felt a sudden impulse to scream. Something large and heavy rustled awkwardly through the ferns. Fear, like lust, swelled within him. He felt a loathing and a horror and, inexplicably, a sense of expectation as well, almost as if some small part of him yearned for what it knew was about to take place. He began to sob. How could he escape from this thing - how could he possibly even hope to escape from this thing - if some perverse element within him did not want him to be free?

He turned around to retrace his steps up the glade, but there was something dark stretched across his path, barring his way, some yards ahead of him. It turned towards him and rose. Starlight, filtering through the trees, glittered darkly across its teeth as it smiled.

Lamson turned around and tried to run back down the glade, but the creature was already bounding after him like a great black goat. He felt its claws sink into his shoulders as it forced him forwards, knocking him suddenly face down onto the ground. He tried to scream, but his cries were gagged on dried leaves and soil, as his mouth was gouged into them. The creature's furiously powerful fingers tore at his clothes, strewing them about him. The winds blew cool against his hot, bare flesh as sweat from the lunging, piston-like body ran down the hollow of his spine.

There was a crash somewhere and the dream ripped apart.

The next instant he seemed to blink his eyes open to find the comforting sight of his familiar bedroom in front of him. The book he had been reading when sleep overcame him earlier, lay against his feet on the floor.

He breathed out a sigh of relief as he glanced at his watch. It was three thirty-five in the morning.

He shivered. Covered in sweat, his body felt awful, aching in every joint. He put on his dressing gown and crossed to the window, opening the curtains to look down into the twilit street below. It was empty and quiet, peaceful as it never was during the day. But it was also undeniably lonely. Cold and lonely and lifeless. The sight of its bleak. grey lines could not make him forget the dream for long, nor keep him away from the wretched feeling of despair that remembering it brought along with it, a despair made all the more unbearable at the realization that its cause, deep down, must lie rooted in his character. There was no way in which he could deny to himself the perverted aspects it presented to him. But was he perverted as well? Or had the old tramp been lying? After all, he reasoned, why should he be any more perceptive of that kind of thing than anyone else? It was the man's horrible suggestion, and that was all - no more certainly! - that was making his mind work in that direction now. Almost, he thought, pensively staring about his room, like some kind of post hypnotic suggestion. And if this were so and it was the tramp's vile insinuations that had caused this neurotic and evil obsession, then it was up to him to vent these desires in the most normal way that he could. Otherwise, he knew, they would only worsen, just as they were worsening already.

Decided on this course, he rested quietly for the rest of the night, reading through the next few chapters of *Over the Bridge*, and listening to the radio.

When the sky began to lighten at last, he welcomed the new day with a fervor he had not felt for many weeks. At last it seemed to him as if there was a chance of ridding himself of this nightmare.

At last...

*

It was not till midday that he dressed and stepped outside.

In realizing that he had to prove to himself that he was normal and rid himself of the perverse obsession that was deranging him, he had decided that the easiest way open to him was to call on Clara Sadwick, a local prostitute who rented rooms on Park Road above a news agent's shop. As he walked towards it down the sodden street the place appeared to have a dingy and slightly obscene look to it, with unpainted window frames and faded curtains, pulled together tight behind their grimy, flyspecked windows.

As he stepped inside and began to climb the bare staircase to the first-floor landing, he gazed bleakly at the mildewed paper on the walls. A naked light bulb swayed on the end of a cord at the head of the stairs. He wondered what he had let himself in for at a place like this. Fortifying himself, however, with the thought that in going through with what was to follow he might end the dreams that had been tormenting him for the past three weeks, he pressed on the buzzer by the door facing him at the top. One fifteen, she had said on the phone when he rang her an hour before. It was just a minute off that time now. He ran his fingers nervously through his uncombed hair.

After a short pause the door opened before him.

"Believe in punctuality, don't you?" Clara said with an offhand familiarity which made him feel more relaxed as she stepped back and looked at the slim gold watch on her wrist. She was dressed in a denim skirt, fluffy red slippers and a purple, turtle-necked sweater which clung about her ample breasts.

She smiled as she showed him in.

"Make yourself at home," she said breezily.

"Thank you," Lamson said as he hung his coat on a hook by the door and looked about the room. In the far corner, partially hidden behind a faded Japanese screen, was a bed. In front of the old gas fire stood a coffee table crammed with dirty plates. He wondered if she had been having a party or whether, as seemed dismayingly more likely, she merely washed them up when there were no more clean ones left. He hoped, fleetingly, that she was a little more conscientious about cleaning herself.

Clara ground the cigarette she'd been smoking into a saucer, then said:

"It'll be forty quid. Cash first, if you don't mind. It's not that I don't trust you, but 1 can hardly take you to court if you refuse to pay afterwards."

Lamson smiled to cover his embarrassment and said that he understood.

"You can't be too careful, can you?" he added, sorting out the notes from his wallet. "Forty pounds, you said?" he went on, as he placed the money in her waiting hand.

"Many thanks," she replied, taking it to a drawer and locking it inside.

She looked back at him coyly.

"Well, I suppose we had better begin," she said, folding back the screen from the bed. With no further words, she kicked off her slippers and began to unbutton her skirt. Within a few minutes she was dressed only in her tights and bra. She looked up then as if only just remembering his presence and told him to hurry. "I haven't all day to wait for you getting undressed. Unless, of course, you prefer having it with your clothes still on." She shook her head, laughing almost like a young girl, though she was in her late thirties, unfastening her bra and letting it fall forward from her breasts. Lamson swallowed as he stared at the limpid mounds of pale white flesh that were uncovered, their puckered orbs matching the goose flesh that was starting to rise on her cozily rounded arms.

She shivered, complaining to him again at his slowness.

"Do you want me to help you?" she asked sarcastically.

Lamson shook his head as he loosened his trousers and let them fall, unaided, to the floor. Stepping out of them onto the lukewarm oilcloth he looked at her again.

"Come on, luv," she said as she rolled back on the rumpled bed. "Off with the rest of them and we can begin."

Although Lamson felt embarrassed at his nakedness as he slipped out of the last of his clothes, and could feel the blood burning through his cheeks, he was surprised - and not just a little alarmed - that there was no other reaction, that he seemed, in fact, to be incapable of carrying out what he had paid for. Seemingly unaware of this - or, if she was, taking no apparent notice of it - she smiled as he approached her. Lightly, questingly, her hands felt about his body as he pushed his face into her breasts. He smelt the faint aroma of sweat and eau-de-cologne, his mind whirling with haphazard and conflicting sensations. She pressed his mouth against her hardening nipples as he moved further up her body. Yet, still, he could not find the desire to possess her.

"Come on, come on, dearie," he heard her whisper between gasps. He raised himself onto his elbows and looked down into her face. In the same instant her hands grasped hold of him between his legs. He gasped as her fingers lengthened and tightened gently about his penis, guiding him towards her. It was as if his loins were being instilled with a surcharge of life.

He looked down at her eyes - Joan's face seemed to merge with hers, hiding the cheapness and vulgarity that had been there a moment before. It was almost angelic. Never before had he looked upon a face such as this, upon which all his pent-up emotions of warmth, affection and even love could be gladly poured. His eyes passed lingeringly about her warm, soft cheeks where the blood made a pleasant suffusion of pink. She smiled encouragingly, and yet with an apparent innocence which drove him into an almost unbearable desire to possess her. He felt her thighs rise on either side of his legs, pressing him to her. He could feel himself grow stiff, entering her slowly, cautiously passing into the warmth within her summoning body. He could have cried out at the exquisite pangs that were racing through him, obliterating conscious thought.

Even through the pleasure that was overwhelming his mind, though, Lamson became suddenly aware that the room was darkening. Something sharp and dry scraped painfully across his back. He cried out in alarm as it stuck, like a vicious hook, ruthlessly dragging him away from her.

The pain crescendoed suddenly as he was tugged from the bed and flung onto the floor. Contorted in agony, he looked up. He glimpsed something dark stride over him. There was a scream. It seemed to cut deep into his ears like slivers of glass, and he tried desperately to crawl back onto his knees. Then the screaming stopped, as suddenly as it began. Instead there was a ripping sound, like something being torn apart.

"No! God, no!" he sobbed, dizzy with nausea, his sight blurring as he seemed to start falling in a faint. Whatever stood over him still moved, its weight shifting from one leg to the other in sickening, horrifying rhythm to the rips and tears from the bed.

Feebly Lamson tried to reach out across the sheets to stop whatever was going on there, when something soft and warm touched his fingers.

Something wet.

It clung to him as he automatically recoiled away from it, screaming hysterically as darkness closed in all about him.

*

It could have been hours, or even just minutes afterwards, when he opened his eyes once more. However long he'd been unconscious, the tawdry bedchamber had gone, as if he had never been there. Instead he was stretched out on the floor of his flat, facing the window. A blowfly buzzed aggressively, though with result, against the windowpane. Besides this there was silence.

As he slowly climbed to his feet, his first reaction was one of intense relief. He could have laughed out loud in that one brief instant in joy at the fact that it had never happened, that it was all just a horrible dream, that he had never even left his flat! Then he noticed the spots of blood on his shirt. There were scabs of it clotted about his hands and fingers. His stomach heaved with revulsion as he stared down at the ugly stains covering him like the deadly marks of a plague.

"Oh, my God!" he muttered, rushing convulsively to the sink to wash them from him. His hands still dripping, he grabbed hold of his shirt and tugged it from him, grinding his teeth against the pain in his back as the scabs swathed across it were torn open. His shirt had been glued to him by them. When the pain subsided enough for him to touch them, he gingerly felt across his back, his fingers cautiously trembling along the blood-clogged grooves gouged into him. Crestfallen with horror, he stared at his haggard face in the mirror above the sink. Did it happen? Was it not just a dream but some vile distortion of reality?

He stepped back into his bedroom and looked at the head, perched where he had left it. The thing stared at him with its coal-black, swollen eyes. It seemed bigger than before, like an oversized, blackened grapefruit. You know, he thought suddenly, you know what happened, you black swine of a devil! But no, this was madness. How could he believe that the thing had some sort of connection with what had happened? It must be something else. But what? he wondered. What but something equally bizarre, equally preposterous could account for it?

What?

What?

Outside he heard the two-tone siren of a police car as it sped down the road. After it had gone there was another. Lamson strode to the window and looked down as an ambulance hurtled by, its blue light blinking furiously.

He leant against the windowsill, feeling suddenly weak. Resignedly, he knew that it happened, it really did happen. By now they must have found her blood-soaked body, or what was left of it. He gazed down at the stains still sticking to his fingers and wondered what he could do. Like the Brand of Cain, threads of blood clung to the hardened scales about his knuckles. If only he had thrown that stone away when he'd intended to originally. If he had, he was sure that none of this would have ever happened. He grabbed hold of the stone, clenching it tightly as if to crush it into dust. Something black seemed to move on the edge of his sight. He turned around in surprise, but there was nothing there now.

He placed the head back on the dresser and took a deep breath to compose himself. He wondered if he had left it too late to get rid of the head. Or was there time yet? After all, there was no saying what the thing might make him do next. Reluctantly, he looked again at the head. How he wished he could convince himself that it was nothing more than just an inanimate lump of stone. Once more he picked it up, his fingers experiencing the same kind of revulsion he would have felt on touching a diseased piece of flesh.

"Damn you," he whispered tensely, suddenly flexing his arm. There was a movement by his side, furtive and vague. He whipped round. "Where are you hiding?" he asked shakily, searching round the empty room. There seemed to be a sound somewhere, like the clattering of hoofs. Or was there? It echoed metallically, almost unreal. "Come on, now, where are you hiding?" Something touched his arm. He cried out inarticulately in revulsion. "Go away!" he choked, retreating to the window. He turned around to look outside, raising his hand and glancing at the head clasped tightly in his fingers.

Steady, now, steady, he told himself. Don't lose your grip altogether.

He coughed harshly, feeling the phlegm in his throat. It

167

involuntarily dribbled from his lips and spilt on the floor. Looking down, he saw a string of blood in it. He closed his eyes tightly. He knew what it meant, though he wished fervently that he could believe that it didn't. He wished that he could have known earlier what he knew now and done then what he was about to do, when it wasn't already too late.

"God help me!" he cried as he tugged his arm free of the fingers that plucked at him and flung the stone through the window. There was a crash as the glass was shattered, and he fell to the floor.

Something rose up above him, seeming monstrously large in the gloom of his faltering sight.

*

"Are you going up to see Mr. Lamson?" the elderly woman asked, detaining Sutcliffe with a nervously insistent hand.

"I am," he replied. "Why? Is there something wrong?" He did not try to hide his impatience. He was nearly half an hour late already.

"I don't know," she said, glancing up the stairs apprehensively. "It was late this afternoon when it happened. I was cleaning the dishes after having my tea when I heard something crash outside. When I looked, I found there was broken glass all over the flagstones. It had come from up there," (she pointed up the stairs) "from the window of Mr. Lamson's flat; his window had been broken."

His impatience mellowing into concern, Sutcliffe asked if anyone had been up to see if he was all right.

"Do you know if he's been hurt? He hasn't been too well recently, and he might be sick."

"I went up to his rooms, naturally," the woman said. "But he wouldn't answer his door. On no account would he, even when I called out to him, though he was in there right enough. I could hear him, you see, bumping around inside. Tearing something up, I think he was. Like books, I s'ppose. But he wouldn't open the door to me. He wouldn't even talk. Not one word. There was nothing more I could do, was there?" she apologized. "I didn't know he was ill."

"That's all right," Sutcliffe said, thanking her for warning him. "I'll be able to see how he is when I call up. I'm sure he'll answer his door to me when I call to him. By the way," he went on to ask, turning around suddenly on the first step up the stairs, "do you know what it was that broke the window?"

"Indeed, I do," the woman said. She felt in the pocket of her apron. "I found this on the pavement when I went out to clear up the glass. It's been cracked, as you can see." She handed him the stone. "Ugly looking thing, isn't it?"

"It certainly is." Sutcliffe felt at the worn features on its face. It was pleasantly soap-like and warm. He wondered why Lamson should have thrown something like this through his window. "Do you mind if I hold onto it for a while?" he asked.

"You can keep it for good for all I care. I don't want it. I'm certain of that, Lord knows! It'd give me the jitters to keep an evil-looking thing like that in my rooms."

Thanking her again, Sutcliffe bounded up the stairs, three at a time. He wondered worriedly if Lamson had thrown it through the window as a cry for help. Just let me be in time if it was, he thought, knocking on his door. "Henry! Are you in there? It's me, Allan. Come on, open up!"

There was no sound.

Again, he knocked, louder this time.

"Henry! Open up, will you?" Apprehensively, he waited an instant more, then he took hold of the door handle, turning it. "Henry, I'm coming in. Keep well away from the door." Heavily, he lunged against the door with his shoulder. The thin wood started to give way almost at once. Again, he lunged against it, then again, then the door shot open, propelling Sutcliffe in with it.

"Where are you, Henr- " he began to call out as he steadied himself, before he saw what lay curled against the windowsill. Shuddering with nausea, Sutcliffe clasped a hand to his mouth

169

and turned away, feeling suddenly sick. Naked and almost flayed to the bone, with tears along his doubled back; Lamson was crouched like a grotesque foetus amongst the blood-soaked tatters of his clothes. His head was twisted round, and it was obvious that his neck had been broken. But it was none of this, neither the mutilations nor the gore nor the look of horror and pain on Lamson's rigidly contorted face, that were to haunt him in the months to come, but an expression that lay raddled across his friend's dead face which he knew should have never been there - a look of joyful ecstasy. And there was a hunger there, too, but a hunger that went further than that of mere hunger for food.

THEIR CRAMPED DARK WORLD

It was obvious that something was wrong the moment they entered the empty house.

For a start off, it felt far from empty.

There were sounds everywhere.

"If those're rats, I'm out of here," Lenny muttered, his enthusiasm dampened suddenly by the scutterings that seemed to cascade all around them as they walked across the bare floorboards in their trainers. Lenny, the younger of the two boys by barely a month, was tall and gangly, with a livid rash of acne across both cheeks. His dark eyes glanced suspiciously about the ballroom-sized entrance hall as they paused inside it, listening.

Pete grinned. It was a broad, unmistakably roguish grin that somehow made him look older than his fifteen years, as if he'd been born before and could still remember far too much of a disreputably colourful past life.

"Rats are the last things you should be worried about here, Lenny." He made a long, haunting moan that echoed eerily through the house.

"Bollocks," Lenny retorted, anger mixed with the stirrings of doubt he had begun to feel as soon as they approached the old, abandoned house. Making plans was one thing. Carrying them out was something else, especially after dusk had darkened the two acres of woodland around the house into a motion-filled blackness of half-seen, menacing shapes. "We should have set out earlier," he grumbled as he switched on his torch. "Besides, I bet none of the others turn up."

"They'd better," Pete said. "This lot cost me a fortune. Especially since I had to pay that old wino, Karl Ott, to buy them for me." He lugged the rucksack he'd been carrying off his shoulders and lowered it to the floorboards. There was a clink of

171

glass: two half bottles of vodka and a bottle of rum, with a mixture of cokes, Sprite and orangeade. On top was a box of candles in case the electricity in the house wasn't working.

Lenny tried the light switch and the two boys were surprised when the electric chandelier above their heads came on, though half its bulbs were dead or missing.

"The rest of the gang should be here in another half hour," Pete said. "I told them half five."

In late October, though, it was dark not long after four. Now, with heavy clouds covering what little there was of the moon, it was all but black outside.

"It would have been better if we'd all come together," Lenny grumbled.

"What, and miss out on getting into the party mood beforehand?" Pete brought out one of the bottles of vodka and a couple of glasses. "Coke or Sprite?"

Lenny grinned. "Coke."

He accepted the brimming glass and sipped the dark, fizzy liquid inside it. "I can't taste anything but coke," he complained. "Did you pour in some vodka?"

"You saw me, dummy. Fifty-fifty. My dad says you can't taste vodka anyway. Only what you mix with it."

"Then what's the point?"

"You'll see the point when you've drunk it. When was the last time you got a buzz off cola?"

Dubious, Lenny drank some more. "I think I see what you mean," he said a moment later.

"Here's to Halloween," Pete announced, raising his glass.

"Shouldn't we wait for the others?"

"What for? We can have another toast then. There's no law to say you can only toast something once. Come on, hurry up. We've time for a few more drinks before they get here."

Draining his glass, Lenny handed it back to Pete for a refill. Somehow the creaks and scratchings inside the walls and in the ceiling didn't quite seem so menacing anymore. He felt a mild glow start to grow inside him.

172

"It's not hard to believe what happened here, is it?" Lenny said a few minutes and a third glass of vodka and coke later. The warm glow had now spread throughout most of his diaphragm.

"Did you ever doubt it?"

"Naw. But sometimes you wonder whether your parents enjoy embroidering it all a bit just to get you frightened. It's kind of sick, isn't it? A whole family slaughtered, one by one."

"It was worse than that, Lenny." The two boys were sat on the floor in the hallway, the surrounding doors into the other rooms still closed, sealed with festoons of dark grey cobwebs. Most of Pete's face was in shadow as he leaned forward over his glass of coke.

"What d'you mean, worse? What could be worse than that?"

"Worse, 'cause they weren't just slaughtered. They were sacrificed, Lenny, one by one. Whoever killed them, tied them up first so they couldn't move, then taped their mouths so none of them could cry for help. Or hear their screams as he worked on them."

"Worked on them?"

"They were tortured to death, Lenny. It took hours. All night long it went on. There was blood everywhere. That's why there are no carpets. They were drenched in it. Ruined. Even the floors were awash. If you look hard enough they say you can still see some of the stains."

Lenny squirmed uncomfortably on the wooden floor, as if he could feel the old dried blood beneath his buttocks on the dark floorboards.

"You're joshing me, aren't you?"

"Why should I do that? It's all for real. You could check it yourself if you wanted to. It's there in the papers. Every last word. Twenty-five years ago to this night. On Halloween. And no one has ever been arrested for it."

Lenny reached for another drink from his glass.

"Whoever did it must be getting on now. If he was only in his twenties then, he'd fifty now. Sheesh!"

"Fifty's not old," Pete said.

"My grandparents are fifty - and they're old."

Pete laughed. "Bet they'd be pleased if you told them that."

"But it's true," Lenny insisted. "It's too old for a murderer. Isn't it?"

"You're a scream, Lenny. A real scream. Did you know that?"

Lenny grunted.

"Anyway, it's a long time ago."

"And this house is still empty."

"Not always," Lenny said. "I remember people living here."

"Maybe, but none of them ever stayed for long. That's what I mean. None of them," Pete added with an air of significance.

"Are you telling me this place is haunted?"

"Don't you think so? Isn't that why we're here?"

Lenny shivered; his hand reached out instinctively for the vodka and coke. "Where are the others? They should be here by now."

"They'll be here. There's plenty of time yet."

"But it's nearly six."

"And so?"

Lenny shrugged. "It's nearly six. That's all I said. I thought at least one of them would've been here by now."

"Perhaps they've chickened out? Perhaps they know too much about what happened all those years ago and are frightened to come here tonight."

Lenny stared at him. "You're joking, aren't you?"

"Maybe." Pete grinned, that same roguish, all-knowing grin he always used.

Lenny drank some more vodka and coke. He felt a little light-headed now.

"What'll we do if they don't come?" he asked.

"We'll have a party of our own."

"That'd be fun," Lenny said, sarcastically.

Pete merely grinned.

"You did tell them all, didn't you?" Lenny asked a few minutes later. The noises within the walls were still rustling disconcertingly all about them and he was beginning to feel nervous again despite the effects of the vodka.

"Of course I did."

Lenny peered at his Timex. "It's ten past now. Why aren't they here?"

"Perhaps they've chickened out, like I said. Perhaps there's only you and me with the balls to come here."

Lenny reached for his glass. He wished he felt as tough about being in this place as Pete. But the non-stop sounds of hidden movement made him think too vividly of nasty, vicious swarms of rats inside the walls, of scores, perhaps hundreds of the verminous creatures hidden behind the dark wallpaper and wafer-thin, damp-riddled plaster, only feet away from them. With sharp teeth and sharper claws.

"You feeling a bit jittery?" Pete asked.

"Naw..." Even to his own ears, though, Lenny's reply sounded weak. Unsure.

Pete laughed, quietly.

His laughter was beginning to get on Lenny's nerves. He wondered if Pete had really invited the rest of them here. But why would he have lied about this? It didn't make sense.

Unless, Lenny wondered, Pete had some secret reason for wanting to be alone with him here tonight which Lenny would never have agreed to if he had known about it. Unless, Lenny thought, with a sudden shock of insight that left him feeling nauseated, Pete fancied him in some way.

Lenny looked at his friend. Was it possible that Pete was secretly queer?

He didn't look that way. But could he be sure? He knew so little about that kind of thing, and what he did know was probably a load of nonsense. He was only too aware how talk about stuff like that got distorted, with all sorts of myths and rumours and misinformation. Perhaps Pete was gay. He'd a bloody strange grin, that was for sure. And he didn't seem at all concerned that none of the others had turned up tonight– as if he had known all along there would only be the two of them here.

Lenny reached again for his vodka and coke, though he wasn't sure if drinking any more of the stuff was a good idea.

"Are you worried?" Pete asked.

"About what?"

"About this place. About its history. About what went on here twenty-five years ago. What else did you think I meant?" Pete narrowed his eyes.

"Nothing," Lenny said. "Just what you said. What happened here. The murders."

"Bloody gruesome, eh?" Pete laughed. The sound echoed through the empty house and for the briefest of instants Lenny was sure the rustling ceased, as if whatever was making the sounds had heard him and paused - to listen.

"I think I've had enough of it here," Lenny said suddenly. "If the rest aren't coming, it's going to be a bloody bore. We might as well go home and watch TV."

"You chickening out too?"

"I'm here, aren't I? I wasn't scared to come here. I'd have stayed here too if there was any point. But two of us doesn't make a party, whatever you say. And now it's getting cold and there's nowhere to sit except on the floor. And I don't care much for those rats."

"What rats?"

"Those fucking rats scuttering inside the walls, for God's sake. Can't you hear them too?"

Pete shrugged. "To be honest, Lenny, I'd forgotten about them. Got used to the sounds, I suppose. Just background noise. White noise, don't they call it? Anyway, they're harmless. Have you ever heard of anyone you know being attacked by rats? They're only aggressive if they're cornered. Everyone knows that. Leave them alone and they'll leave you alone. It's as simple as that."

"So you're an expert on rats now?"

Pete frowned, his grin gone. "Have I upset you, Lenny? Have I said something to annoy you? To piss you off?"

"No."

"Sounds to me like I have. Sounds to me like that's why you want to leave. We've not even been here an hour yet. There's still plenty of time for the others to arrive."

"Bollocks. None of them are coming. They'd have been here by now if they were. At least one of them would have turned up."

"You trying to imply something?"

Lenny shrugged. "Maybe."

"Like what?"

"Just leave it. I'm fed up with this place. And that vodka's making me feel sick."

"*Like what*, I said, Lenny?"

"Fuck it." Lenny got to his feet. "I'm off."

"Like fuck you are." Pete stood up too, his aggression obvious to Lenny. What good humour he'd had before had gone. There was a dangerous tautness about his face, which disconcerted Lenny. He had never seen anything like this about his friend before. It was almost as if he had found himself alone with a stranger.

"What's up with you, Pete?"

"Up with me?" The teenager smiled. It was a tense smile, as unlike anything he would have normally given as a grimace. There was no humour in the expression. There was no humour in it at all.

Feeling suddenly afraid, Lenny abruptly made for the outside door, but Pete moved even more quickly, cutting him off, as if he had half expected him to do what he did.

"Not so fucking quick," Pete snarled. He swung a fist at Lenny's face. It was so unexpected that Lenny could barely react before he felt Pete's knuckles crack like a heavy mallet against his jaw. The next thing he knew he was falling, dizzy with shock, nausea and a sudden sense of unreality, as the floorboards loomed against the side of his face. Almost at once Pete was astride him. The weight of his body forced Lenny down onto the hard floorboards, winding him. Still dazed, Lenny felt his hands being pulled in front of him. Something thin was tugged tight

177

around his wrists, forcing them together. He struggled to sit up when he saw that a narrow strip of plastic, like the kind his father used for tying up plants in their yard, was being pulled around his wrists, then locked into place. He tried to push it apart, but the plastic tie was far too strong and cut his skin.

"Pete! What are you doing?"

His friend reached into one of the pockets of his jacket and pulled out a roll of gaffer tape. He tore off a six-inch strip of it, held it for a second above Lenny's face, as if gauging his target, then tugged it tight across his mouth. Lenny tried to scream, but his lips couldn't move beneath the vile-smelling tape.

"That's better," Pete said, finally. He eased himself up, then stepped back, grabbed a hold of Lenny's feet and forced them together. Before Lenny could do anything to resist him, another, heavier plastic tie had been secured around his ankles. It was so tight it hurt as it bit into him.

"Had enough?" Pete asked.

Lenny tried to say something, but his lips were squashed beneath the unyielding tape gummed across them. The skin around them felt as if it would tear if he tried to force them open.

"Resistance is futile," Pete said, grinning once more, his voice familiar to both of them as a Borg from *Star Trek*. The sudden humour sounded misplaced and false to Lenny as he uselessly struggled against the plastic ties around his wrists and ankles and realised just how painful it was to try to snap them.

"Do you think our unknown, unscrupulous friend, all those years ago, used plastic ties and gaffer tape to immobilise *his* victims?" Pete asked. "He might have had gaffer tape, I suppose. It could have been around then. I don't know. I don't suppose plastic ties were, though. Do you?"

Pete turned, retraced his steps to the pack he'd brought their drinks in and squatted down to search inside it till he found what he wanted, then slowly rose to his feet once more, a look of triumph on his face. Lenny squirmed on the floor to watch him, his heart thumping so loud in his ears it almost blotted out the rat-like scratchings inside the walls. Deep grunts of panic came from inside his throat when he saw the knife Pete held in his hands. He fondled it almost like he would a pet as he stared at Lenny over it. It gleamed like very expensive steel. And its edge looked sharp.

"Bet he'd have given his high teeth for something like this," Pete said. "Cost an arm and a leg. Paid for it with my dad's credit card on the internet. But he buys so much expensive crud using it he'll never notice one more item he never bought himself."

Pete pointed the knife at Lenny's face, clearly enjoying the sight as his friend's eyes opened wide in abject terror, staring back at it, unable to look away.

"You know, Lenny, I often think I've been here before. Somehow I've always felt like that. My mother told me that when my gran first saw me as a newborn baby, she said, "He's been here before, this one. He's been here before." D'you know that, Lenny? Even my gran recognised this wasn't my first life. It's not my second, either. I've been here lots of times before. Lots and lots of times." He took a step nearer. "And every time I've been here, I've had this task, this very important task to do, to ensure I'll be able to come back again. I've done it so often over the years it comes to me in my dreams, time and time again, as clear as I can see you now, to make sure I can't ignore it." He hunkered down beside Lenny's head. "But I'd never ignore it. That's why there's only you and me, why no one else was told about us coming to this place tonight. No one knows we're here, Lenny. It's a secret. A secret between you and me. And you'll never tell, will you, Lenny?" Pete snickered. "That's a bit of a no brainer, if ever there was one, I know, but I couldn't resist it." His hand flicked out and the point of the hunting knife sliced a line across Lenny's forehead. Lenny would have screamed at the sudden, intense pain, as a trickle of blood pulsed out of the cut and dripped into one eye, but the gaffer tape kept his straining lips gummed together.

"Shush, shush," Pete whispered. "I've not begun yet. There's someone here you've yet to meet before the real thing starts." He cocked his head to one side. "You've heard it, though. That scuttering." Pete stood up. Behind him, from the wall, Lenny saw something move where the old wallpaper seemed to hang open now like a dislodged curtain. From beyond it, something large and grey, like a huge, misshapen rat moved out into the light of the room. There were others, smaller, huddled behind it. Their dark eyes, gleaming like soiled rubies, stared at Lenny.

"They like the blood," Pete said as he crouched beside him again. "Especially Him. He's old. So old you couldn't imagine it. He was brought to this place so long ago, too, when I was in a different body, with a different name. So long ago even I can't remember what name I had, there've been so many in between. But it doesn't matter. What does is His power. That's old as well. As old as the world. Perhaps older. When others like Him were plentiful. When they ruled. As one day, if Mankind has its suicidal way and we destroy what we have of this world, He'll rule again."

Lenny struggled to scream as he watched the creature move across the floorboards, as large as a pig, its ugly, scaly rat-like face etched with countless sores and wrinkles. Most of the thick grey hair had fallen away from its corpulent body, baring the glistening skin beneath. If he had not been gagged, he would have shouted at Pete that he was mad, that this ugly creature wasn't what he seemed to think it was, but some insane monster that had fooled him. It wasn't godlike. It wasn't godlike at all. Just some pathetic old demon. How he sensed or knew this, he wasn't sure. Instinct, perhaps. Some old race memory from a time when things like this had flourished. He didn't know. All he knew with certainty was that Pete had been taken in by it. That it needed him to provide it with the worship it craved - it and its hideous, ugly children.

Though rat-like in shape, as it moved out into the light, Lenny realised the thing had no mouth as such, just tubular, fleshy tendrils. Each, though, ended in what *looked* like a mouth - mouths that opened and closed as it slowly, furtively moved towards him.

Again, Pete sliced at Lenny with his knife, cutting deep into one of his hands. Blood pulsed from the wound. And the rat-like creature moved in, its tendrils dipping into the blood as it spread across the floorboards. Lenny's body tensed with horror and disgust as he heard the hideous slurping sounds from the tendrils as they sucked at the pool of blood. And the other, smaller, rat-like creatures scuttled forwards, drawn by it.

In sheer desperation Lenny struggled to free his lips from the gaffer tape, chewing at what snippets he could draw between his teeth. He fought against the pain as Pete sliced away his jacket and t-shirt so he could make further gashes in his body.

"Part of it is your pain," Pete told him, as if this expiated him. "He needs to feel that – that and your fear. He feeds off them both."

Several times during the next few hours Lenny blacked out, either from nausea or pain or both. Each time Pete waited till he was conscious again, then started once more, cut after cut, till the floor surrounding them was thick with blood. The other creatures had moved in on the pool as it spread across the room and had begun to feed from it.

Almost too weak from blood loss to feel much pain any more, it was only then that Lenny was able to force his mouth open. The gaffer tape was sodden with spit and weakened where he had gnawed at it.

But by then he could barely talk, let alone scream for help, and Pete merely glanced at him as he carved more cuts in his chest.

"Pete…" Lenny's voice was a ragged croak, barely intelligible. "Pete…"

"Too late to plead for your life, Lenny. Far too late for that, I'm afraid. *He* must feed. And so must they. I'm held to do it. I always have been. And always will."

"*Twenty-five years ago,*" Lenny whispered. "*You did it twenty-five years ago.*"

Pete glanced down at him, smiled, then moved the knife speculatively across his friend's abdomen.

"You're fifteen now. How long did your old self live after what he did here?"

Pete shrugged. "How long is a piece of string, Lenny?"

Midnight had come and gone, and still Pete worked, his face lost in the intensity of it. Lenny died not long afterwards. And as he died, so the blood flowed slowly, then stopped.

Pete looked around at the creatures. *His* creatures. *His* Gods.

The large one stared up at him from the blood it had been drinking.

"I've served you well," Pete said. "Again." He smiled, roguishly.

Something heavy moved across his foot. He looked down and saw one of the smaller creatures climb across it. Others milled around his ankles. And for a moment he felt uneasy. But it was always like this. They were thanking him for what he had done for them.

The large one, *his God,* stared up at him, though, its dark red eyes unwavering as it moved towards him. There was more to be done. Just what, he was unsure. But there was more, he was certain. He felt himself being pushed by the others, their bodies as big as well-fed cats. Then he remembered. This was his moment of rebirth – the moment he would enter the darkness of the void. The moment he would leave this shallow husk till the time was right to return. Ten years he had hung in the void before till he entered this body. His time to let go of this body was now.

Was now.

Pete screamed as his God lunged at him. It claws dug deep into his chest, as it dragged him back towards the gap within the wall. The others scrabbled about his feet, biting and nipping and scratching him.

"No!" Pete screamed as he remembered it all, all those times in the past. He had to go with them now, into their cramped dark world. But he didn't want to go into that void again where they would feed off his flesh and blood, revived and hungry.

His final act of sacrifice.

"Till next time," he heard himself scream in despair.

As his eyes stared in horror at the grim darkness between the walls where they were dragging him.

Where he would feed and sustain them and make them fat for years to come.

Also available from
Parallel Universe Publications

BLACK CEREMONIES
by Charles Black
ISBN-10: 0957453558

THE HEAVEN MAKER AND OTHER GRUESOME TALES
by Craig Herbertson
ISBN-10: 0957453517

GOBLIN MIRE
by David A. Riley
ISBN-10: 095745354X

THINGS THAT GO BUMP IN THE NIGHT:
A TREASURY OF CLASSIC WEIRD
edited by Douglas Draa and David A. Riley
ISBN-10: 0957453566

HIS OWN MAD DEMONS:
DARK TALES FROM DAVID A. RILEY
ISBN: 978-0-9574535-8-6

THEIR CRAMPED DARK WORLD AND OTHER TALES
by David A. Riley
ISBN: 978-0-9574535-9-3

Check our website:
http://paralleluniversepublications.blogspot.co.uk/

www.ingramcontent.com/pod-product-compliance
Lightning Source LLC
Chambersburg PA
CBHW070932250626
47159CB00009B/3217